DEAD AHEAD

His fingers itched for the feel of the bills. Twenty-five big ones. A lot of green. He could make it grow, live easy for the rest of his life. "Let's see it."

The gloved hand reached into the pocket and then surfaced. It was too dark for Frankie to make out the gun. Two massive blows struck his stomach. He fell to his knees, then onto his side. His insides felt as though they were on fire. Something smashed against his temple, exploded.

It was the last thing he felt.

———————

DEAD AHEAD

RUBY HORANSKY

AVON BOOKS  NEW YORK

This is a work of fiction. Names, characters, places, and incidents either are the product of the author's imagination or are used fictitiously. Any resemblance to actual events or persons, living or dead, is entirely coincidental.

AVON BOOKS
A division of
The Hearst Corporation
1350 Avenue of the Americas
New York, New York 10019

Copyright © 1990 by Ruby Horansky
Published by arrangement with Charles Scribner's Sons, Macmillan Publishing Company
Library of Congress Catalog Card Number: 90-33076
ISBN: 0-380-71653-4

First Avon Books Printing: July 1992

AVON TRADEMARK REG. U.S. PAT. OFF. AND IN OTHER COUNTRIES, MARCA REGISTRADA, HECHO EN U.S.A.

Printed in the U.S.A.

RA   10 9 8 7 6 5 4 3 2 1

For Joe

ACKNOWLEDGMENT

Sincere thanks to my friend Bob, a Detective Sergeant in the New York Police Department for the past seventeen years, who answered dozens of questions cheerfully and generously. I am deeply grateful for his time and help.

The goddamn wind—Frankie was almost frozen. Warm all fall, and tonight it had to turn bitchy and start raining. He hunched into the jacket, dug his hands deep into his pockets, and kept walking.

One more block to go. Why did it have to be set up here, in the ass end of Brooklyn? He barely knew where he was, behind the motel on the stretch going down toward the marinas. No man's land. Wet grass, dead tires, hardly any traffic. It was almost a quarter to, he figured. He had to be there by eleven.

He'd make it—if he didn't freeze his balls off first. Why the hell couldn't someone have lent him a car tonight—just this once? He'd tried his friend Arnie, his boss, his brother, Pete. He'd sworn he wasn't going to the track, but no one believed him anymore, that was the trouble. So he'd ended up on the bus—*two* buses. Twenty minutes waiting to transfer, water running inside his collar, soaking his shirt. Well, after tonight he wouldn't need to borrow a car. He'd have enough to buy ten cars if he wanted.

But he'd start with one. A red Ferrari. One of those babies could go ninety and not even steam up. He pictured himself behind the wheel. He wasn't a bad-looking guy; the broads would go for him. It was worth it, hiking out here to the middle of nowhere. All that loot. It would give him a new start.

He came to the end of the block and there it was, a diner where you'd never expect one. A little bitty thing, all covered up with high grass on this side. Closed now. Sad looking, one of those places the owner might burn down for the insurance, stuck out at the end of the world. They'd named it right—Land's End Café.

He shivered a little, chilled by the damp and the look of the place. Why'd the meeting have to be here, so far from civilization? He should have said something maybe. The whole scene gave him the creeps, reminded him of when he was in Vietnam. He'd be on patrol and come across a deserted village—you were never sure if all the VC snipers had been cleaned out till you walked through it.

He hesitated before he turned in, chewed a hangnail. It was too late to back out now. He'd go, keep the date the way they'd set it up. Why worry? He was going to come out a winner. He just wasn't used to the way these things were done.

When he had the money he'd get rid of these crappy clothes. Tomorrow he'd throw away these rags and buy everything new, join a gym and start working off the flab. But first he'd get some solid bets in—invest the money to make sure it *made* money. After all, if you put together your own system for the ponies you had to believe in it, didn't you? You had to back yourself. He could parlay this pile into big numbers, six figures, maybe.

He'd buy lots of presents—fancy sweaters for Arnie and Pete, a toy for the baby downstairs. He liked kids. Maybe he'd even find a broad who'd put up with him, have some kids of his own.

He'd show everyone he wasn't so dumb. Pop had always been after him to get a regular job. A sucker job, nine to five. But there were better ways to live. Some people were lucky; they had it easy. Last night he'd finally had a real lucky break.

The right place at the right time. Last night had been the turning point of his life. Just luck that he'd been in that particular spot. Now he'd build on his luck—he was smart enough to know how to follow through.

He picked his way through the garbage cans set out on the side, feeling excited as he got closer to the money. It was a lot of dough, but they hadn't hassled him. They'd agreed to it. It had gone smooth, almost too smooth. He felt a shiver of uneasiness again, pushed it down.

He had to go all the way around the place to find the parking lot.

And then it was empty.

He'd expected to see someone sitting in a car, waiting for him. Jesus, what if he'd come all the way the hell out here for nothing? They wouldn't back out, would they? They wouldn't dare. Still, he didn't trust them.

A noise behind him made him turn.

A figure stood in the shadows.

Frankie squinted, walked closer. "You bring the money?"

"Yeah."

His fingers itched for the feel of the bills. Twenty-five big ones. A lot of green. He could make it grow, live easy for the rest of his life. "Let's see it."

The gloved hand reached into the pocket and then surfaced. It was too dark for Frankie to see what was held in the hand. Mercifully, for he had no time to make out the gun, anticipate the bullets. Two massive blows struck his stomach. He fell to his knees, then onto his side. His insides felt as though they were on fire. He heard footsteps come close, stop next to his ear. He groped for his attacker's legs and touched air. Something smashed against his temple, exploded.

It was the last thing he felt.

Nikki Trakos pulled the Plymouth up to the yellow crime scene ribbon stretched across the diner parking lot. It was just another day, she tried to tell herself, an ordinary working day. Yet she didn't believe it. This was the first homicide she'd caught since she'd become a detective. She felt as excited as a racer lined up for the marathon, eager to prove herself, show what she could do. She'd wanted this for as long as she could remember, had dreamed about it through her academy training, her years on patrol, her time in Public Morals. Hold it down, she cautioned herself. Just do your job.

She eased her long legs out of the Fury and slammed the door. Two uniformed police stood guard—Bernardi, with whom she'd partnered once or twice, and a female rookie, looking like a teenager with her ponytail tied under her cap.

The kid looked green around the gills; she must've had a look at the body. Nikki remembered how sick she herself had been the first time she'd seen a corpse, ten years ago, on her first patrol assignment. The body had been a "stinker," had lain undiscovered for days in a two-family house in East Flatbush, an old black man who had died of a heart attack. Nikki, twenty years old and fresh out of the academy, had been the first one through the door, hadn't even covered her mouth as her partner had, and had thought as she first inhaled the stench of days-old death that she too was going to die. She'd barely made it to the toilet to throw up everything she'd eaten for a week.

"Hi, sugar." Bernardi leered at her. He was pushing forty, a Don Juan who tried to make it with every woman who crossed his path.

"*Baby*," Nikki cooed. It made her laugh whenever he came on to her. At six feet she towered over him, as she did over a lot of men. She was tall, broad-boned, generously formed. He'd become a cop right after the height requirement had been dropped and was only five four. He was starting to get paunchy. She felt like Snow White with one of the dwarves.

It was still early, about 0800 hours, damp and mist drifting in off Sheepshead Bay though the rain had stopped. A gull shrieked overhead. She could just about make out the World Trade Center towers and the lower Manhattan skyline through the haze. She knew this stretch of land, not just from her police work but from her childhood. Her father had been captain of the *Poseidon*, a boat that took sport fishermen out for the day. Nikki, strong and tall like the son he'd always wanted, had served as his mate on weekends and school holidays.

She turned to Bernardi. "You first officer on the scene?" It was funny to ask the question instead of having it asked of her. She'd been a detective only two weeks—it was hard getting used to it. Detective Investigator; a beginner.

"Yeah. The guy that owns the place called nine-one-one. He found the stiff when he come in at seven."

"How about EMS?" If there was any doubt of death, Emergency Medical Services, the city's ambulance corps, would be called.

"He don't need EMS. He needs an undertaker."

She pointed toward the lot. "Who's been inside?"

"No one. We kept it clean."

"Good. I'm going to take a look."

She ducked under the ribbon and felt her adrenaline charge. Her first homicide. There were so few murders in this precinct—maybe five or six a year. It was just luck that she'd caught the case.

She felt high on that special feeling her work gave her. Was it true, as her mother kept saying, that she was using work as a substitute for "real living"—by which she meant a husband and family? "An unsettled head sleeps in a cold bed," her mother wrote in all her letters, translating the Greek proverb. An unmarried thirty-year-old daughter was cause for deep concern. She'd become a *yerodokori* —an old maid. Now that Nikki had adopted her niece, Lara, and was raising her, she had lessened her chances of finding a husband, had thrown happiness out the window.

The wind whipped her ankles as she turned a corner and walked deeper into the lot. The white paint that marked the parking spaces needed renewal. A frayed broom and a string mop kept each other company near peeling wooden steps that led to what must be the diner's kitchen entrance.

The body lay near a rusty dumpster behind the diner. Because of where it was they hadn't covered it—nobody could see around the building. She wanted to be alone with the corpse right now, study it before the Crime Scene Unit arrived and did its measuring, photo taking, sampling, and scraping, absorb her own impressions while everything was still intact.

She stood above the man and felt a shudder in her stomach; it had been a while since she'd seen a corpse.

As homicides went, he wasn't that messy. He lay on his

side, arms outstretched, hands reaching. The pool of blood around him had formed a broad oval.

She circled him carefully. Then, avoiding the blood, she bent for a closer look.

Between forty and forty-five, stockily built. Too much fat, most of it around his belly. Rough, not unattractive features. Thick brown hair streaked and stained by blood from a temple wound. Lots of blood.

Down on his luck, to judge by his clothing. Thin gray slacks with seams pulling; a tear at the corner of his jacket pocket. Scuffed, mud-covered shoes. No drag marks visible. That, and the abundance of blood, made her believe this was the scene of the murder. If he'd been killed elsewhere and dumped here, there wouldn't have been half the blood. Bleeding stopped at death.

The flow was dry now, stiffened on his clothing and congealed on the asphalt. Wide around his middle, could have a stomach wound or two. If not for the red-stained clothing and the hole in his head, he looked almost as though he'd tripped and fallen, reached out so someone could help him up. But he wasn't going anywhere, not anymore.

Anger filled her. Who had done this to him? Why had his life been wasted? Whoever he was, whatever he'd done, he didn't deserve this.

She took a pocket camera from her purse and shot a roll of film, careful to get him from every angle. The Crime Scene Unit would take pictures too, but these would be hers, would help her remember the body as she'd first seen it.

She walked back out toward the street, pulled a small spiral-bound book out of her bag, and began taking notes. She would make him a DCDS—Deceased Confirmed Dead at Scene. Across the ribbon she saw the rookie looking at her with new respect. Years ago Nikki had heard her Uncle Spyros, the detective, say, "I always use a book, even if I doodle in it. You look like you mean business."

Bernardi's eyes were cruising up and down Nikki's legs, checking their length, the shape of her calves, the diameter of her ankles. Nothing stopped Bernardi; if the man were assigned to disaster duty, he'd still be climbing over every female in sight.

She'd worn sensible pumps today, not because she was worried about the extra inches high heels would add to her already imposing height but because she never knew where her work would take her, how fast she'd have to move, whether she'd be standing on her feet for hours. Sensible pumps and her brown-and-white tweed coat. She tried to compromise between the pretty and the practical, add a touch of something flighty. This morning, Lara had picked out the earrings with the clear blue stones—"They match your eyes, Aunt Nikki."

Bernardi finished his inspection, grinned appreciatively. "Tall, tan, and terrific."

She fluttered her lashes in mock rapture.

"Meetcha later?" he asked.

"Sure, lover. If I don't show up, start without me." She turned her back on him. "What's your name?" she said to the rookie.

"Cook."

Nikki glanced up and down the street, remarked, "Pretty quiet."

"Yeah, we're lucky. Four, five blocks over, by the houses, you'd have people three deep fighting for a look." They stood on a stretch of land used mostly as a run-through to the Belt Parkway or the big shopping mall. No cars had stopped, though traffic was beginning to build.

A rain-spattered Buick sat in the lot. "Whose is that?" Nikki asked.

"Belongs to the owner." Cook pointed to the diner. "The waitress and busboy came by bus. Want me to do an auto canvass?"

"Thanks." Cook would list the plate numbers of cars parked on the street so Nikki could interview their owners later.

"Waste of time," Bernardi put in. "There's three cars on the whole strip, and one of them's a junk heap. Wouldn't leave my car here unless I wanted it to disappear."

She walked out to the curb. The nearest building was a city water-pollution plant three long blocks away. In the other direction, even farther, stood an abandoned construction site. Whoever had picked this place for a murder had chosen well. An auto canvass might give her a little to work with, a canvass of witnesses nothing.

She was pretty sure the man had been killed right here. Which suggested that he'd been taken for "a ride," gangland style. Yet the murder didn't look like a professional execution. It wasn't neat, for one thing. And the wise guys had a way of making their victims disappear; they didn't leave bodies around for the cops to work on. The other possibility was that the dead man had met someone here. Funny place to set up a meeting.

She went back for another look, this time searching for spent cartridge casings or telltale items that might be important later. No casings at first glance. It seemed likely a revolver had been used—fired casings were stored in the chamber of the revolver, not ejected. Maybe there were casings under the body; she wouldn't know until it was moved. She stood over the corpse for a long moment, then bent to study the head wound.

"What the hell d'you think you're doing?" A man's rasping voice, unmistakably that of her supervisor, Lieutenant J. J. Parcowicz—"Eagle-Eye" to the detectives who worked for him—boomed across the lot. He was striding toward her. His pinched nose made his face look thinner and bonier, gave him a permanently inquisitive look.

He didn't want her on the squad. Ever since she'd been assigned, two weeks ago, he'd made that clear. It wasn't Nikki particularly—it was any woman. "This is a man's job," he'd said on her first day. She'd wanted to ask, *In what way?* Did he think men had more brains or guts than women? How would he know whether a woman could do the job—he'd never had a female on the squad before. But she'd contented herself with a simple, "Yes, sir." The best way to convince him of her worth was to prove herself.

If only he'd let her work! He'd been fussing over her like a rooster with a new hen, coaching her on exactly how to lay eggs. She wasn't used to it; it made her feel like a specimen under a microscope.

"You're not supposed to be in here yet, Trakos," he said now.

All the detectives on murder cases she'd seen had gone in before the Crime Scene Unit, to size it up, get a feel of the case. The bastard enjoyed giving her a hard time, got off on it. "I'm securing the scene, sir."

"Securing bullshit. Destroying it, probably."

She stifled an urge to tell him to fuck off. Her last boss, Cashman in Public Morals, had ignored her—hoping maybe she'd go away. For three years he'd left her on her own, waiting for her to foul up. But at least he'd left the day-to-day stuff up to her—as long as she closed out cases and cleaned up her files.

Eagle-Eye glared at her across the corpse. "Only an asshole would be in here *before* the Crime Scene people. Don't you know that?" His voice was loud enough to carry out front—the story would be all over the squad room tomorrow. "I could have you up on a Command Discipline, Trakos."

He bent to look at the body. Nikki wanted to point out that he too was in violation of procedures, but she felt this wasn't the moment to mention it.

He glanced up, squinted at her. "Don't get too excited about the case—I'm taking it away."

"Sir?"

"You heard me. Maybe four, five homicides in this precinct every year. I've got to be nuts to let you have one. You're too green."

She could feel heat stinging her cheeks, spreading to her ears. "But we catch in rotation—I was up."

"I don't care where you were. It's my job to see that cases get solved. I can reassign whatever I want."

It was true; he had the right. But she couldn't let it happen. "Sir, how do I get experience if you won't let—"

"That's what they call your problem, Trakos."

He straightened. In another minute he'd be gone and so would her big case, her opportunity.

She swallowed hard. "I wonder if people will think you took it away because I'm a woman."

She had his full attention now. Let him wonder whether she'd press sex-discrimination charges, stir up a fuss. "Sir, I'm asking you for a shot. Give me a limited time, and if I don't come up with answers, then take it away."

He was chewing on it, trying to turn the rusty wheels of his brain. When he spoke, his mouth was so tight it hardly moved. "Three days, Trakos. That's what you got."

"Thank you, sir."

"Don't thank me. Come up with the perp."

"Yes, sir."

His tone became businesslike. "Crime Scene Unit?"

"On its way, sir."

"Under the new system there's a hotshot coming in to team with you, a specialist."

"So I heard." Each local murder had to have a detective

from the special homicide squad assigned to it. She'd been itching to show her *own* strengths, prove to Eagle-Eye what she could do. "Sir, whose case is it technically?"

"Yours. But I don't want to hear any shit that you aren't working with the guy. You stay inside police regs, or I'll stomp on you."

"Yes, sir." He'd be watching her every inch of the way anyhow.

"The guy's name is Lawton. Should be here any minute." He started walking back toward the ribbon, stopped abruptly. "Remember, Trakos—three days."

"Yes, sir."

He got into his car, his forehead knotted into a series of ridges. He glared at her, massaging the bridge of his nose with the tip of a finger as though his sinuses hurt. She watched with relief as he sped away.

Three days. It wasn't an eternity, but maybe she could do it.

While she'd been gone, three blue-and-whites had angled into the ribbon. A crowd of uniforms clustered near Bernardi and Cook. Mitchell, the husky white-haired patrol sergeant, walked toward her.

"Hey, Nikki—how's the new shield? They miss you in PM—Cashman's lost without you." He reminded her so much of Uncle Spyros, sounded like him, and even looked like him, with his square face and dark eyes. Her uncle, long gone, had been her childhood hero. She remembered his visits, could picture him sipping wine and eating honey-nut sweets and telling her about his nightstick, his walkie-talkie, explaining how they were used. If only he could know she'd taken on her first murder case today—how proud he would have been!

"How you doing?" Mitchell asked now.

"Okay." She tried to keep her excitement under wraps.

Somehow it seemed indecent to have this bright-eyed eagerness because a man had been murdered.

She looked at the knot of uniforms in front of the ribbon. "I haven't seen so many cops since the mayor's birthday party," she said.

"They all want a look. A little action after the noise complaints and traffic tickets."

"Do me a favor—keep them out of *there*." She pointed at the ribbon.

"Sure," Mitchell said.

A blue-and-white station wagon, the Crime Scene Unit vehicle, turned the corner of the diner and pulled up. Two evidence technicians got out, a short, dark, heavyset man and a tall blond one with glasses and lightly pockmarked cheeks. She'd seen them before. The blond one's name was Meekins; she couldn't remember who the dark one was.

Meekins unwrapped a stick of gum, shoved it into his mouth. "Okay, what've we got?"

"An unhappy customer," Bernardi said. "He complained about the chicken salad and the owner blew him away."

"Very funny." Meekins chewed loudly with his mouth open. "So who caught the case?"

"I did," Nikki said.

She felt his glance slide over her, saw his smile dry up. "Okay." He looked away. "Let's see what this one's about."

She followed as they ducked under the ribbon. They moved in for a look at the body, surveyed the area, checked for anything significant on the ground. Meekins pointed to the head wound. "That one looks like it finished the job." He looked at Nikki. "Anything special you want?"

For a moment she wavered. There was a difference in watching detectives take charge of murder cases over the years and taking charge of one yourself. Like driving a car after you'd been a passenger. But this was the day she'd been waiting for, wasn't it? She shook off her uncertainty. She told Meekins what evidence she wanted, made notes in her book so she'd remember for her reports.

She watched them set up. Neither said a word to her. They seemed unrelaxed because she was there. She walked back to the ribbon.

A gray Chevy Caprice angled toward the lot. The man who got out was in his late thirties or early forties, with a bright, compelling look that drew her attention. Unusually large eyes, alert and intelligent, dark hair above a high forehead, a face full as a cherub's. But a wise and knowing cherub, one who'd had experience in the world. All his movements, the way he walked, the gestures of his hands, were quick and impatient.

He looked around. "Detective Trakos?"

"That's me."

"Dave Lawton, Homicide."

Her specialist partner. Something about his name clicked in her brain but she couldn't quite place it. She saw his glance travel over her swing of brown hair, register her blue eyes, rangy shoulders, unusual height. He was only a few inches shorter, stockily built but athletic—a man who took care of himself. Nikki had come to terms with her size long ago, lost the sense of awkwardness she'd had as a girl. Yet it was hard to shrug off Lawton's gaze, the penetrating brown eyes measuring her. She tried to remember what her grandmother used to tell her. "Nikki, *glikia mou*"—calling her "*darling*" in Greek—"God loved you so much He made lots of you."

Lawton gave her an easy, slanted grin. "Always like to work with top-level people."

The teasing bothered her. Was he uncomfortable having a woman as a partner—trying to lighten it? Whatever it was, she should remind him they were working on a case, not out on a date. She tucked a strand of hair behind her ear, a gesture she caught herself in whenever she was edgy. "The Crime Scene Unit's in the back."

His smile was replaced by a more businesslike look—with a hint of admiration in it? She wasn't sure.

"Good." He held her eyes an extra moment and she found herself wishing they *were* on a date, or in a situation where she wouldn't mind responding as a woman. She was sorry she'd worn her tweed coat. A suit showed off her shape better. What was the point in having a good figure if you didn't show it off?

There was something appealing about the man—the humor lines around his eyes, his easy smile. What was she thinking! She needed all her wits about her today, didn't dare become distracted.

She ducked under the ribbon. Whenever she got a new partner there was the tension of how it would be working together. She and Lawton would be a team only for the life of the case. After that they'd most likely never see each other again. Under this new system a homicide detective was temporarily assigned to a local cop so he could add his expertise to the cop's knowledge of the neighborhood.

Lawton lifted the ribbon, and Mitchell asked, "Are you the same guy who caught the duffel bag case?"

"Guilty." He seemed pleased that Mitchell had heard of him.

She remembered him now. A drug dealer's body had been found in a duffel bag downtown. Lawton had been working the case for months—a detective first grade, a rising star. The Brooklyn DA's office was interested in the killing. The victim had been supplying crack locally, was thought to be part of a larger operation in Queens. Lawton's name was starting to show up on TV and in the papers.

"Making the headlines," Mitchell commented.

"Getting ulcers," Lawton said.

Nikki followed him around the corner.

Meekins looked up and grinned. "Dave, you son of a bitch! Whatcha doin' out in the boonies?"

"Same thing you are. Got it solved yet?"

"Sure. We can all go home."

"Wish I could," Lawton said. "They got me swinging by the nuts. Too many cases." He bent for a look at the corpse, then straightened. "I need this one like I need a case of the runs." His sports jacket was cut from a rich brown plaid and fit his solid shoulders as though it had set him back a week's salary. Some detectives were peacocks. They earned well and were so glad to be out of uniform they splurged on trendy, expensive clothes. She liked nice things too, but with a child to raise she had to watch her budget.

"What happened with the creep we did for you last week—the one without the ear?" Meekins asked. "You thought there might be a tie-in to the duffel bag guy."

"There was. He was the wife's boyfriend." Lawton stepped back toward the dumpster to get out of the way. "The whole thing's starting to break. My partner's waiting for the widow to get back from Jamaica. I was supposed to be with him—and then *this* came in." He shook his head. "Whoever runs things downtown is missing a few marbles."

She understood his frustration at being dragged off a big case and sent out to this sleepy end of Brooklyn. Compared to the homicide he was talking about, her case was a "little" murder. The guy on the ground, whoever he was, hadn't been a drug lord by the look of him. He probably wouldn't make any papers except local ones, and he wouldn't connect to any larger crime. But she felt troubled by Lawton's attitude. Was it because it lessened the feeling of importance she'd gotten from catching her first homicide? No—there was something democratic about murder; every victim should have the right to a careful investigation.

She waited for a break in the conversation, then said to Lawton, "It doesn't look like there was a struggle."

He glanced up, preoccupied, and studied her a moment. "Oh yeah." He refocused his attention, looked at the body. "That's right. He looks kinda neat, and the blood's in one spot. But it rained last night, it's hard to tell."

Meekins clicked his camera and lights flashed. "He took it close," he said, moving to photograph from another angle, "from maybe three, four feet. Some time around midnight, but don't quote me."

Lawton said to her, "We'll know more after the lab tests and the post." If there had been a struggle, the autopsy might show particles of skin under the nails, even traces of blood.

"Maybe he knew the perp," she said.

"Could be."

She paused. "Were my instructions okay?"

Lawton looked surprised, then checked the Crime Scene Unit clipboard. "Fine."

She had the urge to tell him it was her first homicide but stifled it. He could care less.

He stroked the dark hair above his ear with the flat of his palm. His nails were clean, trimmed. A gold ring gleamed on his pinky. "Listen, I'm going to the diner to make a call. I want to see if they picked up the wife." She was puzzled for a moment, then realized with annoyance that he was thinking about his other case, the big one. "It won't take long."

He was back in a few minutes. "Shit!" he said. "They brought her in and they're starting to question her."

He glanced around the parking lot, at the body lying still and gray on the asphalt. "Look," he said to her suddenly, "you pretty much know what you're doing. I'm going downtown for an hour or so. I'll be back."

Big fucking deal. A publicity hound, chasing after headlines, caught by his image in the media.

He handed her a card. "If you need me, I'll be at this number. See you."

He raced around the diner before she could say anything.

Not that she could think of anything she really wanted to say. She wasn't going to run out to beg him to stay. In any event it wouldn't have changed his mind. Anyhow, why should she need Lawton there—to hold her hand? It was probably just routine police work from here on in. But she was angry. It wasn't fair that he'd raced out here, made a big splash, then dumped all responsibility for the case on her.

She remembered what he'd said and became even angrier—"I'll be back." Who was he kidding? His office was at least a half-hour's drive away, and that was with no traffic. Once he got there he'd be involved with his duffel bag case, and this little murder would slip his mind altogether.

It was clear what his priorities were. Yet if there were a breakthrough on this case, if she managed to solve it, he'd have to get credit. "She wasn't alone—this specialist guy helped her." And if anyone asked how the partnership was working out, she'd have to cover for him, say he was offering full cooperation and assistance. Why should she have to do that? She hardly knew the guy.

The hell with Lawton. She forced her thoughts back to the man on the ground. The caked mud on his shoes caught her eye. He hadn't stepped into it around here—this was all asphalt and cement, except for the small reedy patch next to the diner. Maybe he'd been down at the shore. About a quarter of a mile away across a stretch of divided roadway lay the bay, edged with small sheltered marinas and boat yards, the sport-fishing boats.

She had to remember to ask for a sample of the mud on the shoes for analysis. The body went into the medical examiner's office fully clothed. The shoes and the rest of the clothing wouldn't be removed until the autopsy.

She watched the technicians finish up. No spent casings. No gun. It was unusual to find the weapon at the scene. Still, she'd wanted a lucky break, something to give her a lead. She'd fantasized about her first homicide. She didn't want a grounder, an easy case that came neatly wrapped with an obvious killer, evidence, and clues. She'd wanted to show off a little. But this one didn't seem to have any kind of handle at all. Not yet.

She checked her watch. Ten-thirty. She'd have to call for a baby-sitter to pick up her niece Lara at school. No way she'd be going home—not with a murder breaking. She liked to warn Lara that the sitter was coming, but often she didn't know in advance. Lara acted better when she didn't have any surprises. She'd had enough uncertainty in her nine years.

She pulled her attention back to the case again, watched the technicians go over the lot, check the corners, look into the garbage pails, empty the dumpster. Nothing.

A field of beach grass bordered the diner. Later they'd

spread out and search it. She didn't expect to find anything, but you never knew.

While the Crime Scene techs were packing their gear Bernardi, as first officer on the scene, slipped on a pair of rubber gloves and went through the man's pants pockets, now stiff with blood. Mitchell listed the contents.

Bernardi pulled out an old gray wallet. Nikki was surprised to see it, wondered why the murderer had left it. Definitely not a mob hit. Not their style to leave ID to make the cops' job easier. The wallet was bloodsoaked, worn through in spots. It held a driver's license with a photo on it.

"Francis Sunmann, 4570 Cedar Lane, Brooklyn," he said, giving the corpse a name and identity. "Bensonhurst —my neighborhood." He looked at the photo. "I never seen the guy."

Bensonhurst was twenty minutes away by car, longer by bus. What had Sunmann been doing way over here?

He opened the wallet. "Sixteen bucks—six singles and two fives."

"Not much, but he's still got it," she said. "Whoever it was didn't rip him off."

"Maybe he didn't want to touch him. Guy's a bloody mess." He flipped through the compartments. "No credit cards."

"I have a feeling he never had any. Or if he did, it was long ago."

He reached into the other pants pocket. "Keys and cigarettes. One Bic lighter—not working. Some matchbooks. A piece of paper with a phone number on it and a couple of addresses."

It was half a sheet of lined paper, ripped from a spiral notebook. The phone number had no area code—local, probably. Below, someone had scribbled "Land's End Café," with the address. A second address was listed on the side, with no name.

Inside the breast pocket of Sunmann's jacket was a folded tear sheet from the *Daily News*, "Yonkers Selections," and a plastic-encased snapshot. She looked at the tear sheet. In each race two horses were circled.

"A handicapper," Mitchell said.

A loser, she thought.

She took the driver's license and snapshot. The picture under the plastic showed him in happier days, his arm around a younger, thinner version of himself—a brother, maybe. The transporters loaded the body onto the ambulance for its trip to the medical examiner's office.

Bernardi, Cook, Nikki, and Mitchell pushed aside the tall grass in the field next to the diner. They found pieces of worn tires, an old piston ring, yellowed bits of newspaper, a brown paper bag with an empty fifth of rye—again, nothing that seemed significant. The stuff looked as though it had lain there for years, blown by the wind off the bay or tossed from passing cars. Nikki put a sample of earth into a plastic bag, labeled it for the lab. Maybe it would match the mud scrapings from Sunmann's shoes.

The early morning haze had gone. A pale sun peeked through intermittently, as though it couldn't make up its mind. Bernardi and Cook reported themselves back in service and drove off. Mitchell stopped on his way to his car. "What happened to your boy Lawton, the big specialist?" he asked Nikki.

"He had to go downtown."

She tried to keep the resentment out of her voice, but Mitchell looked at her closely. "Maybe he'll be back," he said.

"Sure—like tomorrow. What'm I supposed to do, wait for this joker? I have to move on this shit."

"Call Eagle-Eye and tell him you're doing a solo."

She wasn't telling Eagle-Eye anything—not if she could help it. If she went to him with the truth—that Lawton had taken off in the middle of an investigation—it would be like snitching. Procedure said you were supposed to tell your superior if a partnership wasn't working out, but how many cops ever did? Women cops least of all. They were edgy about how well they were accepted by male officers to begin with; most of them were careful not to make waves.

She looked at the diner. "I think I'll start. Maybe Lawton'll be back by the time I'm ready to leave," she said, knowing that he wouldn't and angry with him that he'd put her in this spot.

3

She'd need someone to take care of Lara, not just this evening but maybe for the next few evenings. For the hundredth time Nikki found herself wishing there were someone else to help her bring up her niece. Sometimes she thought she'd made a mistake taking her on. Police work didn't mix well with parenting. And Lara had special needs, was troubled by more than the usual childhood fears. Her mother, Nikki's sister, Iris, had died four years ago, leaving Lara insecure and afraid Nikki would leave her too. She wanted her around all the time.

Officially, Nikki's day ended at four. Today was different—she had no idea when she'd be going home. A murder case never fit into a neat schedule. The first twenty-four hours after a body was found were the most important. Go explain *that* to a nine-year-old.

There was a pay phone near her car. She dialed the number of her downstairs neighbor, Mrs. Binsey. The phone rang five or six times. Nikki could picture Mrs. Binsey dragging her bulk off the couch and shuffling toward the phone, one eye still on her soap opera. If Nikki had been able to choose, she would have asked for many qualities in Lara's baby-sitter that Mrs. Binsey didn't have—warmth, expressiveness, empathy for a troubled kid. But she had no choice. Mrs. Binsey was the only sitter she'd been able to find who was willing to work on such short notice. That was because what she was doing—watching television—could be easily interrupted.

She arranged for Mrs. Binsey to pick Lara up at school and went inside. The diner was a shabby place, not like the one owned by her uncle Pete, where her father had worked during winters when he'd been landlocked. Missing tiles made the floor bumpy. The stools were scarred, the counter chipped.

The owner was named Daly, a short, wiry man with a scrawny neck and close-set eyes that gave him an angry look. Nikki sat opposite him at one of the wobbly tables, listened while he told his story. It was simple and straightforward. Yesterday he'd closed at four-thirty in the afternoon, as always. He was the last person out—the waitress and busboy were gone by four. "We do a breakfast and lunch business, then we clean up and close. Of course today I can forget my breakfast trade, and if you don't get outta here soon, I can kiss lunch good-bye, too."

He talked excitedly with his hands. "My whole day's business'll be loused up with this shit. Sorry for the language, miss—uh, Detective Trakos. But you cops're screwing me. When you gonna get outta here?"

"Listen, Mr. Daly. If you don't want to do this at your place, we can always do it at *mine*. Want to come down to the station?"

His shoulders drooped and he glared at her. "It's okay," he muttered.

"Those pails outside are empty," she pointed out. "When was the pickup?"

"Last night."

"About what time?"

"I ain't here when they come."

"Who takes it, Sanitation?"

"No. We got a contract with a company."

"Which one?"

"What the hell d'ya need to know that for? Just a waste of time."

"Talk about wasting time, Mr. Daly, we can do this fast or it can take the rest of the afternoon. I thought you were the one in a hurry." She met his gaze, stared him down. She didn't bother to explain that she had to follow every lead. If the cans had been emptied after the killing, something important might have been carted away in the garbage. "Let's have the name of the company."

Daly rose, his mouth tight with annoyance. He brought back a business card.

She jotted down "Phoenix Cartage Company" and the phone number, handed back the card. "When's the dumpster emptied?"

"Friday. They took it last week."

"When did you last see Francis Sunmann?"

"Who?"

She pointed outside. "The man who—"

"Like I said, when I come in this morning."

"And before that?"

"Never. I *told* you already, I never seen the guy in my life."

"Maybe he ate here—"

"Not regular. I know the people come in regular."

"So you never met him—"

"I just *told* you that."

"Say, thanks for your cooperation," she said, smiling sweetly. "That's all for now. Send in the waitress."

The wooden chair scraped on the floor as he rose.

The waitress was an elderly redhead who looked oddly familiar. She wore a white miniskirted uniform. Her name tag said "Stella." Nikki rummaged through dusty old memories, remembered that the woman had attended St. Spyridon's, Nikki's family's church.

Stella remembered her. "You're Costas Trakos's girl, aren't you? The older one."

"That's right."

"So you became a cop." She was looking at Nikki, openly curious. Would her next question be the inevitable one, about Nikki's marital status? She remembered suddenly that the woman was a gossip, had had one of the most active jaws in the neighborhood.

She was searching for a tactful way to head off her questions when Daly, the owner, snapped, "Give it a rest, Stella, or we'll never get through."

Stella sat down, unperturbed by his bluntness, and answered Nikki's questions. She'd worked there fifteen years, she told her. She'd noticed nothing unusual yesterday, had gone home at four. She didn't recognize Sunmann when Nikki showed her the driver's license photo.

"Of course he coulda come in once or twice. Sometimes we get people from the motel, the Star Garden. You can see it from the window."

The two-story white brick motel building was about five blocks away, partly hidden by the pollution plant. Nikki hadn't realized it was that close.

She took Stella's full name and address, thanked her.

The busboy was an Indian from South America who had been in the country a year and was terrified when she tried to talk to him.

"He's a good kid," the waitress said. "Does his job, never makes no trouble. He lives near me, sends money to his family somewhere. He's scared you're gonna send him back. He left the place with me yesterday afternoon." That had been hours before anything had happened to Sunmann.

The owner was cracking a roll of quarters into his register as Nikki got ready to leave. "Okay," she said, "that's it. If you're planning to go out of town, let us know first."

"What! I *told* you what I know. You're making a whole big deal out of nothing!"

"I've been thinking, Mr. Daly, it wouldn't hurt to come back and question some of your regular customers. Maybe *they* remember something."

"Listen, miss, I'm sorry I gave you a hard time. I had a bad day; I'm in a rotten mood."

She waved her hand to show him there were no hard feelings, but she did make a note about the possibility of interviewing his customers. She'd said it only to keep him in line, but it didn't seem like a bad idea. She couldn't afford to assume anything. She had to keep searching, asking. Yet her gut told her the diner would lead nowhere.

Then why had Sunmann been killed here? Why in *this* parking lot and not any other?

The door slammed behind her as she left. She didn't expect to see Lawton's Chevy outside but looked for it anyhow. Of course it wasn't there.

She dropped a coin in the pay phone and dialed the 168th Precinct. One of the civilian aides answered. She asked to talk to Eagle-Eye, not by that name, of course, saying "Lieutenant Parcowicz, please."

She wouldn't tell him the truth about Lawton. She'd say he'd been called away and she'd ask if he wanted to assign her a temporary partner till he came back.

But Eagle-Eye was unavailable, too. In a meeting. She felt her patience wearing thin.

Call the boss and tell him you're on a solo, Mitchell had advised her.

She *could* wait till Eagle-Eye was free. Yet time was

passing. She thought of Francis Sunmann, sprawled on the asphalt, saw his upraised arms, felt his terror as he was shot. As time passed, witnesses—if there were any—would forget what they'd seen and leads would grow cold. Besides, she had only three days to work on the case. After that she'd be back to burglaries, assaults, the daily grind of squad work.

She asked to be transferred to the Detective Squad, to Jameson, at the desk next to hers.

"Jameson," he answered in his lilting West Indian voice.

"Hi, it's Trakos. Did I get any calls?"

"No, mon." He was always eating some home-cooked delicacy brought to him by one of the cops. Ethnic foods like rolled cabbage or lasagna pleased him most though he had trouble digesting them. She could hear him chewing now.

"What's coming in?" she asked.

"The usual. How's your homicide?"

"Too soon to say. I'm headed for Bensonhurst, where the guy lived. Take the address in case anyone wants me—4570 Cedar Lane."

"Got it." He belched lightly. "Goldberg brought me a jar of pickled herring. Terrific stuff."

"All that crap you're eating is killing you."

"I know, mon, but it's a great way to die. When'll you be back?"

"Not sure. I'll check in again."

She cradled the receiver, took out a map of local Brooklyn streets, and checked the Bensonhurst area. Then she slid behind the wheel of the Fury and zipped toward the parkway.

4

Cedar Lane turned out to be a street where children played and women with baby carriages chatted. In front of the neat brick row house where Sunmann had lived, two tomato plants were staked near a patch of marigolds. Lace curtains hung in the windows.

A thin-faced, dark young woman in a clean housedress answered the door, lost in the long shadow Nikki cut. A year-old baby rode on her hip, its chubby legs outstretched. Its bright-eyed look and round face reminded Nikki of her missing partner, Dave Lawton.

"Does Francis Sunmann live here?" she asked. She showed her badge.

"Frankie, he gotta trouble?" the woman asked in a heavy Italian accent.

"Are you his wife?"

She shook her head. "He liv' upastays. Louisa Bocalli—we owna house."

"Can I come in?"

"Sure."

Nikki followed her across waxed oak floors to the spotless kitchen at the back. Six artichokes lay on a newspaper, earth still clinging to their leaves. Mrs. Bocalli set the baby into its feeding table.

This was the role Nikki's mother had dreamed of for

her—contented housewife and mother, the ideal of Greek womanhood. The trouble was it didn't mesh with police work. She remembered Mark, her first love. They'd been attracted to each other when they were still teenagers, had hoped that when he finished school and got a job they could announce their engagement. Her mother had been ecstatic. He was of good family, a Greek-American, ambitious, would make a fine husband. Problems arose as soon as Nikki started training at the academy. She hardly had time to see him. He was jealous of the male cadets, demanded that she quit and find a "normal" job. Nikki had refused. Recently she'd learned that he'd married someone else, become a father.

She felt a twinge of sadness when she thought of Mark, forced herself now to concentrate on the case again. Mrs. Bocalli gave the baby a rattle, turned expectantly toward Nikki.

"I'm afraid I have bad news about Frankie Sunmann," Nikki said. "He's dead."

Tears filled the dark eyes. "*Morto?*"

"He was killed—shot to death."

Shock and disbelief, but little grief. Her skin looked pasty white. "No! He no fight with no one, Frankie."

"Well, someone must've wanted him dead. Did you ever hear him argue with anyone who came here?"

"No one come here."

"No friends either? How about women?"

She shook her head. "Frankie just come in—he sleep. Once in a while talk'a me. He like'a the baby," she said, a proud smile glimmering through her tears.

He'd been renting from the Bocallis for a year and a half. Nikki asked to see his room and was led up the carpeted steps. Sunmann's space on the third floor was airy and clean. His bathroom was in the hall, but he didn't share it with anyone.

The room was simply furnished. A painted wooden bureau and chair, a bed, a large color TV, the remote control gadget on the nightstand. No phone.

She decided not to go through his belongings just then. She closed the door and applied the police seal sticker to the frame. "I'll take it off when I come back," she told Mrs. Bocalli.

The woman seemed calmer. Sad, but not the way she'd be mourning if she'd lost an intimate. Nikki followed her down the steps, stood near the lace-curtained door. "He paid his rent on time?"

"Maybe once, twice, he'sa—how you say—*in ritardo* . . . late. My husband talk'a him and he get money. From brother."

"Where can I reach his brother?"

"Justa minna." She went into the kitchen, came back carrying the baby and a business card. The baby reached for the card as Nikki took it. It was blue and white, printed, PETE SUNMANN BOAT YARD—MARINE REPAIRS, SLIPS, SERVICE, with a picture of an anchor in the corner.

"That'sa Frankie brother," the woman said.

"Thanks. I'll be back later."

She nodded, her dark eyes large. "He nice'a man, Frankie."

She left Cedar Lane and drove along Eighty-sixth Street. Shoppers crowded the stores. Discounts, drugs, fruit, clothing. Customers fingered clothes on the sidewalk racks, went through boxes displaying bargains.

A train roared by on the elevated structure overhead, cast a shadow on the windshield. She checked the car clock. Three-thirty. How late did boat yards stay open this time of year? She'd head straight to Pete Sunmann's place, try to catch him. She'd call the precinct afterward.

She drove back the way she'd come, along the Belt Parkway, at the edge of Brooklyn's shoreline. The waters in Gravesend Bay were dark and murky. A lone tanker steamed toward New York Harbor while she thought unhappily of what she had to do.

This was the part of her job she hated most, telling a relative someone close had died. She remembered the first time, when she was on patrol. She'd had to tell a woman in a crowded tenement apartment that one of her children had been run over, a four-year-old killed by a car that had jumped the curb. Though it had been nine years ago, she still heard the screams of the mother, the wails and sobs of the kid's brothers and sisters. She'd never forget the peering blank eyes of the grandmother, clutching at her sleeve, too old to understand what had happened. She'd thought that time would help her, teach her how to tell the news so that she was numb to the suffering she caused, but it hadn't.

She left the parkway, drove past yards filled with winter-protected boats, pulled up before a wooden, barnlike structure. The path to the front door had been neatly sectioned off with nautical rope. The red and white sign read, SUNMANN MARINA—BOATS—REPAIRS.

Inside, the smells of motor oil and sawdust blended with the salt tang. Music bounced off the plain wooden walls—Elton John's "Your Song" coming from hidden loudspeakers. A heavyset bearded man stood inside an office, a newspaper spread on his desk. Nikki's glance fell on the article, "Pleasure Boat Explodes—Owner Killed." Some guy out alone on a fishing trip. She'd seen the coverage on TV, remembered it because the dead man, Barry Douglas, had been a wealthy stockbroker who'd lived in her precinct.

She cleared her throat and the man with the beard

looked up, did a double take. "You standing on something?" he asked, grinning.

She was used to the needling, had learned to ignore it. She flipped open her badge case. His face became serious—the ID always had that effect.

"Mr. Sunmann?"

"No, Pete's inside. This way."

He led her through an adjoining room, past racks of black engines hung like carcasses, each labeled with the name of the owner, "Cohn," "Marbelli," "Leuchner." They stepped into an area the height of two ordinary rooms where a boat had been mounted on a wooden platform. A man's denim-covered legs showed behind the keel.

"Mr. Sunmann?"

"Be with you in a sec." His voice was cheerful, deep. The bearded man walked around the keel, whispered something, then left. A second later Pete Sunmann emerged from behind the boat.

She recognized him from the photo they'd found on the body; Frankie Sunmann's face, pared down and younger. He'd grown a drooping cavalryman's mustache since the picture was taken. His eyebrows rose toward the center of his forehead, dipped at the temples, making him look uncertain.

His eyes flicked over her, took a quick survey. He smiled tentatively, seemed uncertain how to respond. He looked behind her. "I thought he said police."

"I *am* a cop. Trakos, from the One Six Eight."

"Oh. Anything wrong?"

She took out the driver's license, showed the photo. "Mr. Sunmann, is this your brother?"

He grew very still. "What happened?"

"I'm afraid I have bad news." Why did it never get easier to say it? "Your brother's dead. I'm sorry."

She watched his reaction, separating the human, feeling part of herself from the cop's observations. Had he known, was he surprised, was he sad? Later these things would be important. Right now she watched. And saw that he'd received a blow. His face seemed to grow even thinner, as though pain were contracting his features.

"How—what happened to him?"

"He was shot."

He stared at her blankly. "I'm sorry. What did you say?"

"Maybe you'd better sit down." If he was faking grief, he was doing a good job.

She followed him into his office, the cluttered room behind the glass windows. He took a fifth of Jack Daniels from the bottom drawer of a file cabinet, poured a few fingers into a glass, and slugged it back, his eyes watering, color coming back into his face. "Drink?" he asked.

When she shook her head he replaced the bottle and kicked the drawer shut. He reached behind the desk and pushed a button. The music stopped, the silence abrupt and empty. "Tell me about it."

"We don't know much yet. He was killed sometime last night, probably around midnight. Someone shot him, left him in the parking lot of a diner not far from here."

His fists clenched. Black motor oil streaked the sleeves of his work shirt. The skin of his hands and forearms were grayed by it. He pressed his palms against the desk, fingers spread. "Stupid schmuck," he said softly.

The outer door banged. A deep voice said, "Police," and then brisk footsteps crossed the entry. A second later Det. Dave Lawton's face appeared on the other side of the glass. She hid her surprise, taking in the dark spots of anger under his cheekbones. His mouth was set, a hard, unyielding line. What was eating him? And how had he found her? She hadn't told anyone she'd be here. He must have gone to Frankie Sunmann's residence, the way she had, and tracked her here with the help of the landlady.

He introduced himself to Sunmann, who still seemed dazed.

She pulled out her pencil and small notebook. "We're going to have to ask you some questions, Mr. Sunmann."

Sunmann frowned. "You said he was shot?"

"That's right."

He shook his head. "It doesn't seem real."

"We'll know more tomorrow, after the autopsy."

He motioned them into chairs, flung himself down heavily. He played with an invoice-stacked spindle on his desk, twirling it between thumb and index finger.

"You close to your brother?" she asked.

His eyes became bright and he swallowed hard. "Yeah. He and I were all— My parents are dead."

"Who was older?"

"He was, but it never seemed that way. He was like a kid who wouldn't grow up." He looked from her to Lawton, then down at his hands again, as though sorry he'd said so much.

Aware of his pain, she waited to ask her next question. She was surprised to hear Lawton say, "Was he ever in trouble with the cops?"

Sunmann looked at the spindle, said nothing.

"You might as well tell us," Lawton said. "Can't hurt him now."

It wasn't Lawton's words but his tone that made him sound so callous. She added gently, "Maybe it'll help find his killer."

Sunmann looked at her. "He was never arrested, if that's what you mean. When he was a kid he was brought in on a gun charge—illegal possession. He wasn't really doing anything. He and his friends were just fooling around. One of my uncles pulled some strings and got it taken off the record. Another time some bums he hung around with wired a car and offered him a ride to the track. When the cops picked them up Frankie was with them. We had to get him out of that one, too. 'I just went along for the ride,' he told me." He laughed bitterly. "The story of his life."

"So he didn't really have a record," she said.

"No. But he made my folks nuts. I think it killed Pop, the way Frankie was. Not that he was bad—just weak. When he came back from Vietnam I offered him a piece of this place, but he didn't want it. Too much work."

"You mentioned Vietnam—was he ever in trouble over there? With drugs, for instance?"

"That was a long time ago. He had a problem, but he stopped. He wasn't really a user. All his trouble ran on four legs. He was always looking for ways to beat the ponies, each one a hundred percent foolproof. He was a big funnel, is what he was. Money went in one end and poured out at the track."

"And when he ran dry?" she asked.

He snorted. "What d'you think? He knew where to come."

"You supported him?"

"No. He drove a car for a service—Patty's, in Coney Island." She wrote the information in her book. "But it wasn't steady, and anyhow whatever he made flew out of his pockets so fast he always seemed to be back here with his hand out."

"You gave him what he needed?"

"Not what he asked for, no. But I took care of him. I paid his rent every now and then, and I'd slip him a few bucks."

"Sounds like a stone around your neck," Lawton said. Again, putting herself in Sunmann's place, she heard the harshness of the tone. Why didn't Lawton ease up?

Sunmann's mouth tightened. "He was a pain in the ass, officer, but I looked after him."

"Detective Lawton means—"

"I know what he means. I didn't kill him, even though I felt like it sometimes. I promised my father I'd take care of him and I did." His mouth drew into a bitter line.

She could have throttled Lawton. She missed the smooth working relationship she'd had with her old partner in Public Morals, Ben Stransky. Ben had been good on details and follow-up, had let her do the questioning because she had what he called a light touch. "You get the whole story," he'd once told her, "without hitting a raw nerve."

"Mr. Sunmann," she said, "I hate to ask you this, but it's routine. Where were you last night, from around ten, eleven o'clock?"

"In bed with my wife."

No way Nikki could check it. People lied all the time to protect their spouses. But somehow Nikki believed him.

"Do you have any idea who'd want to kill your brother?"

"No."

"Any enemies?"

"None I know of. He owed money—he was into the shylocks heavy." Nikki wasn't surprised. It wasn't unusual for a gambler to turn to a shylock, or loan shark, in desperation—someone who asked few questions and would lend money at illegally high interest rates. But mostly shys were patient. If they killed the goose, they wouldn't get any more golden eggs. Once in a while they did make an example of someone who had welshed on a debt. She wondered if that was what had happened to Sunmann.

"How much did he owe?" she asked.

"In the thousands. Never told me exactly."

She was about to ask for the names of the shylocks when Lawton cut in, "You know *who* he owed?"

Damn, it was like playing dodgeball. You had to stay on your toes or you'd get hit. She glared at Lawton, but he didn't seem to notice.

"He never said," Sunmann answered.

Before Lawton could jump in again, she asked, "When did you see him last?"

"A week ago Thursday. He stopped in and said he was short, could I help him out. I gave him a ten."

"Anything unusual about him then?"

"No. But yesterday when he called, he was all excited. Said he had something big going. I figured it was another system."

"He told you that?"

"No. And I didn't ask."

"What time was this?"

"About six, seven at night. He wanted to borrow my car. I said no."

"Did he say why he wanted it?"

"No. To go to the track, I guess."

"He didn't tell you anything else?"

He shook his head. "When I told him no, he hung up."

"Did he have any close friends?"

"One—a guy named Arnold. They bet horses together."

"How about women?"

"He never mentioned any."

"Where can we find this Arnold?"

"I'm not sure. His last name is Greenberg. I think he lives in Brooklyn, but I don't know where."

There must be dozens of Greenbergs in the Brooklyn directory and probably a bunch of Arnolds. She'd need a better lead than that.

She asked Pete Sunmann if he had a recent picture of his brother. He fished in a drawer, came out with a snapshot. "That was two years ago, at the reunion for his platoon." Frankie held a can of Bud, smiled at the camera. "You know he got decorated in Vietnam—for bravery."

"Thanks. I'll return it."

She took Pete Sunmann's home address and phone number, then arranged to meet him at the medical examiner's office the next day to identify the body. "I appreciate your help, Mr. Sunmann," she said.

Sunmann was frowning and didn't seem to hear. "How's the case going to be handled?" he asked. "Who's assigned to it?"

"What do you mean? We both are."

She was about to explain when Lawton said, "I'm from the Homicide Task Force."

Sunmann seemed relieved.

Lawton added, "Detective Trakos is from the local precinct."

Pete Sunmann directed his next words to Lawton. "I want to make sure Frankie gets a fair deal. He may have been just a bum, but he was *my* bum."

"We'll do our best," Lawton assured him. "If it means anything, I've been a detective for twelve years. Homicide's my business."

5

Nikki waited till they were out on the street before she exploded. "What was that last little bit?" she said as they walked toward their cars. " 'Homicide's my business.' What is it for me—a hobby?"

Lawton stopped walking, stared at her. The center of each eyebrow rose in a peak. "What ruffled your feathers?"

"Oh nothing. Just that you made it sound like *your* case."

His eyes narrowed. "You think he'd be happier if I told him it was *yours*?"

"Well, it *is*, isn't it?"

"Sure. But that's not what the guy needed to hear. How many murders have *you* handled?" Lawton's unit, the boroughwide homicide command, dealt only with major homicides.

"What's that got to do with it?"

"I figured you didn't have that many. How would the guy feel if I told him that?"

"How the hell would *I* know," she snapped. "There's something else. If I'm asking the questions, I'll take it from A to Z." His face darkened. A muscle became noticeable on the side of his jaw. "I didn't appreciate your coming in all the time from nowhere. If I miss something, bring it up at the end."

His eyebrows peaked again. "Listen, lady, you're wearing me down. The only reason I came back is because I thought you might need me—or someone. I leave downtown in the middle of a mess, head back to the diner, and where are you? Nowhere. I call in and they tell me you went to Sunmann's landlady. But are you there? No! I have to do as much frigging detective work to find my partner as I do for a regular case. And when I finally get here, you don't like my style. Well, I don't like yours either! Why the hell didn't you stay put or leave word where you'd be?"

"I was at that damn diner over two hours. If you'd come back like you said you would ..." She let the sentence trail off, saw his mouth become a straight, hard line. "I didn't expect you to show—"

"Why not? I told you I would."

"You could've meant next week." She wasn't going to let the scowl on his face intimidate her. "I know where you're coming from. Someday when I'm a star, maybe I'll have something like the duffel bag case, too, and I'll let the little cases slide, save my energy for the big one—"

"Is that what you think?" Even in shadow, his irises glinted like steel. "Listen, hotshot, I do the best I can. If they gave me half the cases, I'd do even better. If you don't like it, tell them. They'll give you someone else, maybe someone you like more."

She turned away from him and looked at the dark waters of the bay, lights clustered near the shore, around the marinas. "I'm not about to tell them anything. If there's one thing I learned on this job, it's how to play ball."

"Then you're stuck with me." He took out his car keys. "I'll be back at my number in a few hours. If you want to talk to Sunmann's boss or anyone else tonight, call. I may have some time."

"Don't do me any big-deal favors." She was sorry the minute she'd said it.

He shrugged. "It's up to you, friend."

She watched him stride to the Chevy. She fully intended to talk to Sunmann's boss and his friend Arnold tonight, but not with Lawton. When she went back to the precinct she'd ask Eagle-Eye if he could spare someone to go with her.

She slid into the Fury. What an arrogant bastard! With any luck, she could avoid him until the case was closed. After that, she'd never have to see him again.

She wouldn't miss him.

6

She was in Bensonhurst again by five, driving on Eighty-sixth Street under the black elevated structure that was part of the subway system. She would put Lawton out of her mind and think of the case again. No way she was going to let personality problems interfere with her work. Not on her first homicide. Screw Lawton. She'd pretend he didn't exist.

Who had had reason to kill Frankie Sunmann, a poor, dumb schmuck who didn't ask much out of life and "just went along for the ride"? Maybe he'd gone along on one ride too many.

She turned off Eighty-sixth, parked on the quiet block where the Bocallis lived, and went up to Sunmann's room again.

The big color TV was the first thing that hit her when she walked in. She saw it in a new light—probably a gift from his brother, Pete, or an impulse buy after a big win.

There wasn't much clothing. He'd been wearing the bulk of his wardrobe when he'd died. A pair of loafers stood in the closet, shined to a soft glow. The polish on the shoes was out of character; she remembered his torn jacket and threadbare pants. And there were no shoe-shine materials in the room.

She went through the drawers. A box full of letters

from Vietnam starting "Dear Mom," dated 1970 and 1971. His mother must have saved them, returned them when he'd come home. No recent mail.

Few items worth looking at. Three joints—he hadn't given up pot completely, not if he kept a supply. A cheap pocket-size address book. Three matchbooks from the Golden Knish in Mill Basin, a delicatessen in Nikki's precinct known for its sandwiches. A single black-covered match folder expensively gold-embossed "The Three Bears—76 Pine Street." An eatery in lower Manhattan, in the downtown financial district. Definitely not Sunmann's turf. She put all four matchbooks into an evidence bag.

She flipped through the address book. There was only one "Arnold," under the As. Was that the right one, Sunmann's friend? He had a Brooklyn address with a phone number listed near it, no last name. She took the address book.

When she was finished, she went down to the kitchen, where Mrs. Bocalli was cooking dinner. The baby lay in a mesh-sided playpen near the table. In the backyard a fig tree had been wrapped and tied for the winter near a small vegetable garden. Nikki remembered the mud on Sunmann's shoes and asked if he'd ever helped in the garden. No, the garden was her husband's, Mrs. Bocalli said. When there were extra fruits or vegetables, they'd given Sunmann some. He was crazy about the figs. In exchange, he'd baby-sit once in a while. He was a nice man; they would miss him. Mrs. Bocalli had straightened up his room from time to time, she hadn't minded.

"And shined his shoes?"

The woman smiled and nodded.

"When did you last shine his shoes?"

"Lass week. Sat'day night."

So the mud on Sunmann's shoes was recent, within the past three days.

Vito Bocalli came home while Nikki was still there. He was a surprise, at least twenty years older than his wife, fiftyish, but strong and vigorous looking. Louisa's face lit up when he walked in. He kissed her and the baby.

Louisa had called him and told him about Sunmann's death, so Nikki didn't have to go through it all over again. She asked Bocalli if he'd noticed anything unusual about Sunmann recently. "He did something funny las' night—no, two nights ago. Sunday. It'sa late—musta be 'leven, 'leven-thirty. He comesa runnin' down, all excited, aska look at the phone book—he gotta no phone, Frankie. Then he'sa run out."

His brother had described him the same way: ". . . yesterday when he called he was all excited." Nikki felt the pieces tumble into place. Sunmann's elated mood could be connected to the murder somehow. "Could I see the book he looked at?"

Louisa ran to a cupboard, brought back a thick Brooklyn directory, laid it on the table. Nikki riffled the pages. No bent leaves, no visible markings. She laid it on its spine to see where it would open, but the pages stuck together and flopped to one side or the other as a whole. Damn it! She wished the print could talk, tell her which page he'd touched, which number out of all these thousands he'd wanted to see. She turned the book over. The cover was clean, nothing scribbled on it. "He looked at it, then he ran out?"

"Yeah, all excited," Bocalli said.

What had gotten him steamed up? A letter he'd received? "Did he get a lot of mail?"

"No, hardly none," Bocalli said.

"How about yesterday?"

"No, he'sa no get letter yesterday. Not for all week, I think."

"What I'm looking for is something unusual—something that would make yesterday different from every other day."

Speaking Italian, Louisa reminded Bocalli of something.

"That'sa right," he said. "Yesterday morning he'sa get call. Frankie, he'sa waitin' for it. He'sa standin' outside his door and he'sa say, 'That'sa for me?'"

"That was unusual? I mean, he didn't get too many calls here?"

"No, never. He'sa talk very low, and he'sa write something. After, he'sa look alla happy, pick uppa baby, dance around. Then he'sa go back upastays. Later, abou' six, seven o'clock, he'sa go out again. Then we don't see him no more."

Nikki asked Mrs. Bocalli, "Yesterday morning, when you answered the phone, who asked for Frankie—was it a man or a woman?"

"Man."

"Young? Old?"

Louisa frowned, then said something to her husband in rapid Italian. He explained to Nikki. "She'sa no know. She'sa never talka him before."

Nikki filled two of the small plastic bags she always carried in her handbag with mud from the backyard. She'd send it to the lab for analysis, have them check it against the mud on Sunmann's shoes.

Her desk was a few feet inside the doorway of the squad room, under the framed dust jacket of a Nancy Drew mystery story that Stransky in Public Morals had given her when she'd been promoted. It showed the girl detective cowering against the wall of a dungeon, pointing her flashlight into its darkness. Cardone, a seasoned detective, had watched while she'd put it up, had gone over to look at it, stood and stared for a few minutes. He hadn't said a word.

In a Lucite holder on her desk was a picture of Lara taken last April, on her ninth birthday. She was leaning over her birthday cake, blowing out the candles, a thin, blonde pixie with a heart-shaped face. With looks like that, why wasn't she popular with the other kids? Yet she didn't have a friend. She ate lunch alone or near the cafeteria supervisor, was never part of the crowd of girls who stayed together all day, whispering and giggling. Once in a while she got invited to do things with the other kids, but she always said no. How long would she live inside her shell? It wasn't normal for a kid to behave that way.

Nikki dialed home. Lara picked up on the first ring as though she'd been waiting for her call. " 'Lo?"

"Honey, I'm working late. That's why Mrs. Binsey picked you up."

"Oh." It sounded like the air going out of a balloon. "When're you coming home?"

"Soon as I can. I'm not sure." Nikki waited through a long silence. "If I'm not there before your bedtime, I'll see you in the morning."

Lara lowered her voice. "I don't want *her* to put me to sleep."

Bedtime was the hardest. Nikki guessed it was because she missed her mother most then. Nikki had played around with different ways of relaxing her before she went to sleep and had finally found something that worked—reading to her from the old book of Greek myths that had been hers when she was a child. But when Nikki wasn't home Mrs. Binsey didn't want to be bothered with a bedtime story.

Nikki swallowed. "Honey, do the best you can. I'll try to call you again, but I can't promise." She'd learned in the four years she'd had Lara that it was better not to promise than to disappoint.

"Okay."

"See you later."

Sometimes she felt Lara would have been better off in Florida with Nikki's parents than with her. She seemed so hungry for attention, as though she never got enough. There were many times, Nikki was sure, when she didn't. And yet when Nikki's kid sister, Iris, had learned she was dying, she had begged her to take Lara.

"Mom and Dad have more time for her," Nikki had said.

"They're too old." Their mother was almost seventy, their father close to eighty. For the first twenty years of their marriage Nikki's parents hadn't been able to conceive a child. Nikki, the "miracle" baby, had arrived when her mother was forty, Iris three years later. "I want *you* to raise Lara," Iris had said.

Nikki felt guilty toward Iris's memory and toward Lara herself every time the girl awakened with a nightmare, each time she saw her alone at school, standing off by herself, away from the other kids. Most mornings she had to convince Lara to go to school. Whatever she was giving her, it didn't seem to be enough. The guidance counselor had told her not to be concerned, that Lara was doing well and would outgrow her fears. But Nikki worried anyhow.

Jameson was shoveling in a load of gefilte fish from an aluminum tray. "Any calls?" she asked.

"The fellow on the burglary case we caught yesterday. He remembered something else missing, a watch." He wiped his lips with a napkin. "I added it to the list."

"Thanks."

"And our lord and master—he wants to talk to you."

"Doesn't he always?" He was probably eager for a progress report. What could he expect so soon?

She glanced at the corner office—his door was closed. His Holiness was in a meeting again. The rule was that no one ever opened Eagle-Eye's door when it was shut.

"How about some fish?" Jameson asked.

"No, thanks. I bought a salad. How do you eat all that stuff and stay thin?"

"I *think* thin."

"Well, I must think fat. All I have to do is smell it and I put on ten pounds."

She put her salad on the desk and unfolded the half sheet of paper that had been in Sunmann's pocket. It had been written by Sunmann—at least the handwriting was the same as that in the address book. The phone number was off by itself and in a different color ink, as though he'd scribbled it first, then added the name and address of the diner and the second address. Or had it been the other way around? Was that the diner's phone number, then—did it belong to the other address or to neither one? She checked it in the directory, but a different number was listed for Land's End Café.

She dialed the number Sunmann had scribbled, but the line was busy, tried again a few minutes later. A recording machine answered, a throaty female voice. "You have reached 555-4529. No one is available to speak with you now, but if you leave your name and number, we'll return your call. Please wait for the beep."

She left a message, waited for someone to pick up on the other end when they heard it was the police, but no one did. She sensed someone was home—the phone had been busy a moment earlier. She didn't want to keep redialing. She called the squad's special contact at the phone company, asked for the source of the number. Their computer was down. They'd call her back when they could check it.

She dialed the Phoenix Cartage Company. They'd emptied the diner's garbage pails at about eight—hours before Sunmann's murder. The crew had noticed nothing unusual about the place.

She opened her purse and took out the matchbooks she'd found in Sunmann's room, examined each one. The glossy black folder from the Three Bears Restaurant was an expensive printing job. She pictured Sunmann's cheap clothes, torn jacket. What would a small-time operator like Sunmann be doing in a power joint like the Three Bears? Still, the fact that he had the matchbook might not mean he'd been there. Matches got passed around like paper clips in this town.

The mud from the Bocallis' yard went to the lab for analysis.

She tried the number she'd found in Sunmann's address book for Arnold. No one answered there, either.

She slipped an Unusual Occurrence form into the typewriter, the report written on every homicide, large robbery, or crime of more than passing interest. She pulled out her memo book and typed the identity of the corpse, her instructions to the Crime Scene Unit team, the apparent cause of death, and a dozen other items. She did a careful job, taking bites of her salad as she worked. The typing went slowly. She'd never been able to pick up speed. After high school her parents had sent her to business school to become a secretary, hoping she'd work for her cousin Achilles, the lawyer. But she'd been bored at business school—been bored everywhere until she entered the Academy.

She rolled out the finished Unusual, reread it, and felt a surge of the same excitement she'd felt in the parking lot this morning. *You are weird, Nikki,* she told herself. Other women were turned on by romantic cruises, singles parties. Give her a nice, solid corpse anytime. She remembered the sadness in her mother's voice last time she'd spoken with her. "Time slips by, my Nikki, and before a woman knows it, she's gray—and alone."

Eagle-Eye opened his door and howled, "Trakos!" He had an intercom on his desk but he never used it.

"Coming, sir." She flung the plastic container that had held her salad at the wastebasket. It hit with a dull thud. Didn't he realize that if he gave her some space, she'd get more accomplished? She picked up the finished Unusual and went into his office.

J. J. Parcowicz sat behind his large metal desk. On the wall to his right was a sign that read THE BOSS ISN'T ALWAYS RIGHT—BUT HE'S ALWAYS THE BOSS. To his left was a bank of filing cabinets. No doubt he collected bits of information on every one of his detectives, had thick dossiers on each.

"So?" he said, fixing her with his intense, narrow-eyed look. He had flounder eyes, she decided, a little bulgy and skewed to one side. "How's the guy from downtown working out? Detective Hotshot what's his name?"

"Lawton." She sat down, adjusted her gun so the muzzle didn't poke into her ribs. "He's helpful," she lied. "Seems to know his stuff."

"Those guys think they're hot shit. How're you making it?"

He didn't really want to hear her troubles, just that everything was going well. "No problem."

"You're lucky. Sometimes it's like a match between my cat and the firehouse dog. I don't know what asshole they have downtown figuring these new systems." He straightened up, leaned back in his swivel chair, and locked his hands behind his head. He sniffed noisily, the sharp tip of his nose curling upward. "What about this homicide— where are we?"

She held out the finished Unusual, but he said, "No, *you* tell me."

She hesitated.

"What's wrong with you, Trakos?" The shine on his nose made it look like a miniature ski jump.

"Frankly, sir, I'm not used to such close supervision. In Public Morals—"

"Well, *get* used to it. Remember, I gave you three days on this thing. I want to know where you are."

For an instant all she could focus on were the words of his sign—". . . he's always the Boss." He didn't have to keep reminding her of the three-day deadline. She could hardly forget it.

She pushed down her temper. "The man was a gambler, sir. He owed a bunch of shylocks."

"That's something to follow." He picked up the Unusual, scanned it.

"Yes, sir. The shys don't like to take out a guy who's paying them, but if he welshes, they'll make an example of him."

"Well, find out."

"Yes, sir, I was planning to. I was hoping to go down and talk to his boss tonight, and one of his friends who—"

He pointed to the Unusual. "The guy worked in Coney Island. You figuring to go down there?"

"Yes, sir. If you have someone to spare—"

"Not tonight." He laid the paper on his desk, scratched the bridge of his nose. "You can't go alone—got that, Trakos? Coney's a jungle at night."

Was he serious? She felt as though she were back in school. "Sir, if I may ask, would you be just as concerned if I were a man?"

"Don't pull that crap with me. You *are* a woman. And you don't even have the protection of the uniform now—as if that meant shit down there. I don't need a Joy Cobb on the squad." Cobb was the first American policewoman to be killed in the line of duty. "How about your partner, what's his name?"

"Lawton."

"He's supposed to be working with you, isn't he? Let him get his ass over here."

Terrific—first tell Lawton to go to hell and then beg him to go with her. She couldn't do it.

He leaned forward, sniffed ominously. "Trakos," he said slowly, "am I making myself clear?"

"Yes, sir."

"And don't get behind on my paperwork."

He'd had no choice about accepting her on the squad —he had to take whatever detectives were assigned. But he didn't have to be pleasant.

"Got that, Trakos?"

"Yes, sir."

"Okay, that's all."

Jameson was swallowing an antacid pill when she got back to her desk. "What's wrong, mon?"

She kicked her swivel chair, sent it spinning. "Is he always up your ass this way?"

He shrugged. "That's his style."

"I'd love to tell him what to do with it." She sat down, stared at Lara's picture. "Meanwhile, what do I do about my case? I have to go to Coney Island to talk to some people, but he says no way I can go alone. I *could* wait till morning—he'll probably have someone free then—but I hate to let it cool."

"Where's the guy you're supposed to be teamed with?"

"You too?" It was getting to be a comedy.

"It's tricky down there, mon. Remember the cop who got shot last month—in uniform, too."

His phone rang, and he turned to answer.

Four, five years ago she would have had no conflict about going to Coney Island by herself, would have run downstairs and been on her way. But since she'd gotten Lara she noticed that she tended to take fewer chances.

She tapped the eraser end of a pencil on her desk, stared at the phone. The thought of asking Lawton for help had as much appeal as having a tooth pulled. After all, she'd turned his earlier offer down cold. She remembered herself saying, "Don't do me any big-deal favors," and felt sick.

It took her a minute to make up her mind. Then she threw her pencil down and dialed.

He answered crisply, with his full name, "Dave Lawton."

"Trakos," she said. Her voice sounded dull and unwilling. There was the tiniest pause. "Ah, my reluctant partner." If he was going to be snide, she'd change her mind and wait till morning. But he said in a businesslike tone, "What can I do for you?"

Her chin and mouth felt tight. She worried that the words would be garbled but forced them out. "If you have some free time, I thought we could go to Coney Island tonight to see Sunmann's boss."

Again, the smallest pause. But this time he said, "Okay. Meet you in an hour, in front of the roller coaster."

"Thanks."

So that's the way crow tastes, Nikki thought as she hung up.

7

Lawton stood on Surf Avenue under the shadows of the giant Cyclone, the old roller coaster that was still one of Coney Island's major attractions. He'd turned his collar up and pulled a soft hat low over his forehead—it made his face seem longer. The hat was a rich dark brown, to blend with his European-cut coat. Straight out of *Esquire*. Compared to him she felt dowdy. She ought to go on a spending spree, buy a whole new wardrobe. Maybe someday she would. She was always catching up with car payments, the baby-sitter, Lara's dental and medical checkups.

Surf Avenue was honky-tonk but well lighted, lined with popcorn and hot dog stands, rides and try-your-skill games. Nikki's first reaction was that she'd been too cautious; she could have come here alone. There were still people on the street, a few couples strolling arm in arm, visiting the amusements, neighborhood people walking home from the subway station on Stillwell Avenue. Then she counted the unusual number of police—foot cops and cruising blue-and-whites—and was glad she was with Lawton.

"How come you called?" he asked as they walked toward Patty's Car Service. "I figured I was on your shit list. Let's see, if I can remember your exact words—"

"Knock it off, Lawton. I had to talk to these people tonight. There was no other way."

He grinned. "Thought maybe I turned you on."

She found herself thinking up an answer, then decided not to respond. The give-and-take between them was distracting, took her mind off the case.

They stopped outside the car service. "How are we going to handle this," she asked, "so we don't step on each other's toes?"

"We'll split 'em. You do one, I do the next."

"Fair enough. You can have Patty's. If there's anything you miss, I'll come in at the end."

That had been surprisingly easy. Maybe he wasn't such a bad guy to work with, she thought as she followed him into the car service. Just a question of getting used to him.

Patty's occupied a storefront and was furnished with a collection of ancient wooden chairs, a rickety card table, a wall-mounted TV surrounded by maps. The squat, burly man behind the card table looked up as they entered, clicked the remote control device at the TV, and turned his scowl on them. She could tell from his edginess that he'd identified them as cops even before Lawton showed his badge.

"You Patty?" Lawton asked.

"Yeah, Patty Lumberman."

"Want to ask you about Frankie Sunmann."

"What about him?"

"He work for you?"

"On and off." He dug at his teeth with a wooden pick held between stubby fingers. "Whadda ya want him for?"

"He was murdered."

Lumberman lifted a thick eyebrow. "No kidding." It would take a lot more to shock this tough old bird. "I ain't seen him in a week."

"That the last time you heard from him?"

"Didn't say I didn't hear from him. Said I ain't *seen* him. He called last night."

"When?"

"Around six, seven."

Lawton pried loose a few more bits of information—Sunmann had tried to borrow a car and had been "on a high." Lumberman didn't know why. In general his answers were reluctant and brief.

Lawton asked if anyone had had reason to kill Sunmann—the shylocks he owed, for instance.

"What shylocks?"

Lawton's tone hardened. "Let's not play games, Mr. Lumberman. We know he owed them. His brother told us. Who were they and how much was he in to them?"

"His brother knows so much, why the hell don't *he* tell you?"

A muscle worked in Lawton's jaw. He leaned forward and spread his hand lightly on the card table. "I don't think you understand how bad I need this information, Mr. Lumberman. Maybe it's time you had your cars inspected. I mean a *real* inspection, where—"

"Okay, sonny," Lumberman said. "He owed two—Teddy and Fonso. They come by to collect and I ask Frankie who are they."

"What'd he say?"

"He tol' me—shylocks."

"He have any trouble with them?"

"How do I know? That's his business. *He* paid 'em."

"Where can I reach them?"

"Who knows?"

Lawton looked at him skeptically, but Lumberman said, "You can inspect what you want, copper. He paid the shys on his own. I don't know where to get holda them."

They were ready to leave when Nikki asked, "Mr. Lumberman, where can we find Frankie's friend Arnold?"

She was so sure he would say he didn't know that she was taken aback when he told them. "The fat guy? He

works by Nathan's, at a place called Sandy's. He's a
dishwasher."

Large, free-flowing tears ran down Arnold Greenberg's
plump features when Nikki told him his friend Frankie
had been killed. They flowed over the ring of blubber
surrounding his face and onto his apron, once white but
now stained with drips of ketchup and other foods. "I
knew something was wrong when he didn't call. I just
knew it."

Sandy's was a snack bar that sold frankfurters, hot
buttered corn, hamburgers, and soft drinks. Arnold had
been ready to sweep when they came in. He'd taken the
chairs off the floor, put four on each table. He took three
down and set them in the sawdust so they could sit. When
he turned his back he reminded Nikki of an elephant, his
huge rear in the gray wrinkled trousers missing only a
tail.

"This is the worst thing that ever happened to me," he
wailed. He opened a bag of potato chips and offered it
around. "See that—I'm eating already. I'm supposed to
be cutting back, but whenever I'm uptight I eat." His eyes
were deep violet, clouded with tears. "This isn't going to
do me any good."

It was a while before he was calm enough to answer
any questions. She didn't have to press him; he was eager
to help.

This was his early night, he told her. One night early,
next night late, that was the pattern. Thursday was his
day off.

"When did you go home yesterday?"

"Late. About eleven-thirty. I didn't get home till four. I
had two of the waiters with me—they live out my way, in

Queens—and the car broke down on the parkway. I had to be towed off."

"Where was that?"

"Right near Springfield Boulevard on the Belt."

"About when?"

"Twelve, twelve-thirty."

"What kind of car?"

"A seventy-eight Ford Mustang. Maroon."

She made a note in her book. If he'd called for assistance, there'd be a report. The waiters had been with him after the restaurant had closed, and the manager and staff could vouch for him before then. That would cover the time when Sunmann had been killed.

"When did you last see Frankie, Mr. Greenberg?"

"On Sunday." His eyes filled again and he reached for another potato chip. "He hung around and waited for me to get off and then we went for deli."

"What kind of mood was he in?"

"Okay, I guess. Nothing special."

"Where did you eat?"

"The Golden Knish, in Mill Basin." She remembered the matchbooks she'd taken from Sunmann's room. "Frankie liked the pastrami."

"What'd you talk about?"

"Nothing much. The track. Mostly I talked and he listened." He gave a sad little smile. "God forgive me for saying it, but he didn't really have that much up here. I did the thinking for us. I remember telling him about a horse I liked in the seventh tomorrow. We were going to go watch it run. I bought him a sandwich, and then I took him home."

"That's all?"

"Yeah."

"Nothing different, unusual?"

"No." He swallowed. Under all the extra fat she could hardly see his Adam's apple move. "That's the last I saw him. Sunday, around ten-thirty."

"Yesterday he was pretty excited about something," Nikki said.

"That's right." His eyes swung to her, the violet deepening. "He called me—sounded like he was on cloud nine. He wanted to borrow the car. 'Arnie,' he says, 'if this pans out, I'm never gonna ask you again. I'm gonna buy the red Ferrari I always wanted.'" The memory brought fresh tears to Greenberg's eyes.

"What was he so high about—a new system for the track?"

"No. He would've told me. And anyhow, he never thought up the systems. They were mine. He just went along. No, this was something else. I asked, but he wouldn't tell me."

"When did he call?"

"Must've been about six-thirty. I was getting dressed to go to work."

"Did you lend him the car?"

"Uh-uh. I needed it to get home and I was afraid he wouldn't bring it back in time."

"He wanted it for the whole evening?"

"No. For a few hours. He asked me could he pick it up at ten and bring it back in an hour or two."

"Anything else he said? Try to remember."

He was silent for a moment, then shook his head.

"Mr. Greenberg, what about the shylocks Frankie owed—how much was it?"

"A lot. I don't know the exact amount, but he was always complaining. 'I'm sending their kids through college,' he'd say."

"Did he ever miss a payment?"

"Yeah, every now and then. I remember once there was a big fuss. One of them called up and threatened him. He thought he was going to end up in the bay. But he must've caught up because he never mentioned it again."

"You don't know which one it was?"

"No, but it blew over, because otherwise he would've told me."

Lawton had a question. "Did Frankie have any enemies?"

"Frankie? No—everyone liked him. He was a sweet guy."

"How about women—was there anybody?"

Arnold grinned, the first real smile she'd seen that evening. "The only women in his life were fillies and mares. At least as far as I know—and we go back a long time. I mean, once in a while he'd go out—someone would fix him up, a one-night stand. But there was never anyone special."

They got ready to leave. "Where can I get hold of the shys Frankie owed?" Nikki asked. "Teddy and Fonso."

"You got me. I didn't even know their names. It was something Frankie took care of by himself."

She expected Lawton to get tough, threaten Greenberg in some way for more information on the shylocks, but he didn't. She was surprised.

She waited, and when they were outside strolling toward their cars she questioned him about it.

"I can usually tell when a guy's holding back and when he's straight," Lawton said. "I'm not always a hundred percent right, but after a while you get a feel for it."

She'd have to use a stoolie to get hold of the shylocks. Sunmann might have been struggling to meet his loan payments, defaulted on a few, and lit a fuse in someone.

The wind blew in off the ocean with deepening cold,

bringing a hint of winter. Nikki buttoned her coat as they walked past a snack stand closing for the night. A thin, dark-skinned girl in an apron wiped the cotton-candy machine.

"You know what sticks in my mind," she said. "Sunmann's change of mood. Here he is, just plain Frankie all day Sunday. And after that he's on a high. His landlord said the same thing—that he came running downstairs late Sunday like his brain was on fire."

"Maybe he saw a chance to make a pile of bread. Sounds like he was in hock to the shys up to his eyeballs."

"Okay, how was he going to swing all this money?"

"If you knew that, you'd probably have the answer to the whole thing," Lawton said.

They walked in easy silence for a while. It was good to stretch her legs, get some exercise. A detective's job had more desk work and sitting around than she liked. All her life she'd been active, worked on her father's boat, played basketball in high school. At one point she'd toyed with the idea of becoming a gym teacher instead of a cop, but it had been no contest, really. The best moments of her childhood had been listening to Uncle Spyros talk about his detective work.

She glanced at Lawton out of the corner of her eye. Tired lines lay below his cheeks, pulled down his mouth. "How's the duffel bag case?" she asked.

"The wife's giving us a hard time. She's grieving more for the boyfriend than the husband, but she's still holding out."

"What's she got?"

"She knows who did them—both of them. But she's scared to say. We've been telling her if she sings, we'll watch out for her. No dice so far."

He slowed abruptly as they approached the amusements. "Hey—I grew up around here. Used to work at one of these rifle stands when I was a kid. Every Saturday and Sunday. I liked the guns."

"You always want to be a cop?" she asked.

"Yeah." He smiled, the grin slanting his face. "Clean up the city, get a medal from the mayor, like in the movies. How about you?"

"I had an uncle who was a cop. He was my hero."

They passed a rifle stand, wooden guns chained to the counter. A sign offered FIVE SHOTS FOR A DOLLAR.

"Want to shoot?" he said suddenly. "I used to be pretty good with these things."

"Sure." At least it was different, a change from the earthier suggestions for extracurricular games made by past partners. She guessed he was a crack shot, wouldn't try it in front of her unless he was sure of his ability. He put down a dollar and the boy behind the counter handed him a rifle. "What's the deal?" Lawton asked him.

"Knock down all five ducks, you win a prize." He pointed to the shelves of bronze statuettes above his head.

Lawton lifted the gun to his shoulder. "It's been a long time since I used one of these." He put his hat on the counter, propped the rifle against his shoulder, squinted through the sight, squeezed the trigger. Four ducks went down.

"Not bad," she said.

"But no prize." He handed her the gun. "Here, you try."

"You're talking to the lousiest shot in the academy. I thought I'd never make cop." She'd passed all the athletic requirements with flying colors but had been shaken by the noise of the gunfire. "What're you afraid of," her instructor had yelled at her, "a big girl like you?" Months afterward she kept dreaming about the firing range, nightmares full of deafening explosions.

"Come on, it'll give you practice."

She laughed. "What the hell." This wasn't the academy, it was just for fun. She sighted along the stock and squeezed off the shots, laughing like a kid when all five ducks fell.

Lawton stared at her suspiciously. "Sure you weren't setting me up?"

"I swear. You must've brought me luck."

The boy said, "You won a prize, lady." He pointed to the statuettes. "Pick one."

"Got any boats?"

He stood on the counter, brought down a schooner with billowing sails. Lara would like that—she could add it to her ship collection.

"How come a boat?" Lawton asked as they walked away.

"My niece collects them. My father makes models. He ran a party boat out of Sheepshead Bay for a long time. My mother and I finally got him to retire."

He smiled his slanted grin. "He must've retired at fifty."

"He had *me* at forty-eight," she shot back.

Gusts of wind lifted the sand under the boardwalk, carried wet spray against her face. The schooner was too large to fit into her bag. She held it under her arm like a football.

"Want some clams?" he asked.

He was easy to be with; she was tempted. She shook her head. "I have a kid at home. I have to get back."

"You married?"

"No, she's my sister's. I'm raising her." She hadn't told many people about Lara's history, but for some reason she felt comfortable with him. "My sister died—leukemia."

"Sorry."

Nikki remembered the hospital room four years ago, Lara waiting near her mother with her small suitcase. Her mind wandered gingerly around that final scene, careful to avoid the sharp spikes of pain. "She was a fighter, my sister. Lara's a lot like her."

Lawton asked, "The father didn't want her?"

"They weren't married—he didn't even know my sister was pregnant. She hadn't seen him in years, wouldn't even tell me his name." She was silent, remembering how ashamed her parents had been, her mother especially. Her daughter had had a child out of wedlock, wouldn't even tell her who the father was. When Lara had come to live with Nikki, Nikki's mother had lied to their relatives, had said Iris's husband had been killed in an accident.

Lawton said, "So you're raising her alone."

"Pretty much. She goes to Florida a few times a year to visit my folks."

She was surprised to see him smile.

"It never works when I beat around the bush," he said. "I meant do you live alone?"

"Yes. No attachments." Why tell him that—it sounded so pointed. She was surprised to hear herself say, "How about you?"

"My wife died years ago. I raised the kids, two of them." The street lamp shadowed his face, making it even more solid, picking out lights in the depths of his eyes. "They're away at school now."

She couldn't think of anything else to say. She twisted a loose strand of hair behind her ear, let the silence grow till they were at their cars. "See you tomorrow," she said. They would meet at the medical examiner's office for the postmortem.

She slipped behind the wheel of her car and gunned the motor. She didn't look back as the Fury shot along Surf Avenue.

8

She drove up Coney Island Avenue, thinking about Lawton, what he'd said. His wife was dead—did that mean he had no current relationship with anyone? Why was she thinking about him anyhow?

She had to pick up her own car at the station house, made a decision to check her desk to see if anything had come in on Sunmann. It was on the way home and would only take a minute. Lara was probably asleep by now anyhow.

She waved to Burke, the desk officer, went up to the squad. Angelo Cardone, detective second grade, sat near the door, talking to a thin young girl whose face was red from crying. A plump, frizzy-haired woman in overtight jeans—probably her mother—burst out, "Why can't you arrest him? He's an animal! She's scared to death to go out on the street."

Nikki pushed past them, went to her desk. It was too soon for the lab reports, but the phone company had called with the information she'd requested.

It lay under her fluorescent, a single sheet. She'd asked for the source of the phone number scribbled on the half sheet of paper in Sunmann's pocket. It belonged to Barry Douglas of Exeter Street, Manhattan Beach.

She'd seen the name in all the papers, as recently as

this afternoon. Douglas was the stockbroker whose boat had been blown up two days ago. She had yesterday's newspaper in her bottom drawer. She dug it out.

An article about the explosion on page four. He'd been fishing a few miles south of the Breezy Point jetty, off Rockaway. For blues, blacks, or maybe early ling. The paper didn't say, but there wasn't much else in the middle of October. He'd anchored and hadn't been able to restart, had called the Coast Guard. The boat had exploded before anyone could reach him. Blown to bits.

The obituary page showed a picture of Douglas. Swarthy as an Arab, thick brown hair combed straight back over a high forehead. His eyes were striking—large, dark, almond shaped.

She skimmed the obituary. "Barry Douglas, of Manhattan Beach, Brooklyn, and Southampton, Long Island . . . forty-two years old . . . A securities advisor with Douglas, Roth Associates . . . survived by his widow, Arden, son, Brian, and daughter by a previous marriage, Denise." She cut out both articles, folded them into her purse.

She studied Sunmann's scribbled note. It didn't make sense. What would a down-and-out guy like Sunmann be doing with wealthy Barry Douglas?

It was too late tonight to approach Douglas's widow. Tomorrow, first thing in the morning, she had to go to Sunmann's autopsy; after that she'd drive out to see Arden Douglas.

She typed a short note to the Communications Bureau requesting information on Greenberg's car trouble. Had 911 received a call for assistance between 2350 hours on Monday and 0100 hours on Tuesday, near the Springfield Gardens exit on the Belt? If so, who had responded?

She sent off the request, left the station, and went to find her car. It was a two-year-old Camaro, the first car she'd ever owned, and she had a love-hate relationship with it. She was wild about the classy blue color and the racing-car look. "Styled with you in mind," the ads had said. But maybe not particularly *her*. It was too low-slung for someone her size. Even now, as she crawled into it, she felt as though she were sitting down on the floor. Once, slipping inside in a hurry, she'd bumped her knee and torn a pair of pantyhose. She'd learned to be careful, get in slowly, but every now and then she forgot. And she hated to take it on long trips. By the time she finally dug herself out, her legs were stiff and cramped, felt permanently bent.

Still, it was all hers—maybe not all, but most of it. And she did love the way it looked.

She buckled herself in, locked the doors, and maneuvered up Coney Island Avenue through light traffic. On Foster she turned right again onto the broad, tree-lined avenue where she lived. Turning off the main street usually relaxed her, made her feel as though she were going back in time. Brooklyn at the turn of the century. Large solid houses under sheltering trees, ample lawns—an earlier, more peaceful period. Bright pumpkins and Indian corn on the porches. Cardboard ghosts and skeletons in the windows to remind her that Halloween was only two weeks away.

But tonight she was too involved in the case to be aware of her surroundings. She kept thinking about the slip of paper in Sunmann's pocket, wondering why he'd scribbled Barry Douglas's address and phone number on it, how recently. He could have been carrying the note for years. Somehow, she didn't think so. She drove along the center divider, a grassy cobble-edged strip strewn with leaves.

She slowed as she approached the house, a solid brown

Victorian with a porch that bellied out like an apron. Right under the roof was a cone-shaped gable, and below that the apartment she rented. She glanced at Lara's window—sometimes her niece sat with her face pressed anxiously against the glass, watching for Nikki's arrival. But she wasn't there tonight.

She pulled into the driveway and opened the garage under the old maple at the back. Though the setting looked benign, almost rural, she remembered this was still the city, with its urban problems—burglary, vandalism, theft. Who should know better than a cop? She pulled in, shut the garage, and locked it carefully.

Upstairs, Mrs. Binsey was watching a game show. "I put Lara to bed," she said. She kept her eye on the TV while Nikki paid her. "Do you mind if I wait for a commercial? I don't want to miss any of the program."

After she'd gone, Nikki turned off the set, made herself a cup of herbal tea, and carried it into the living room. She sat on the maroon velour sofa, opposite the coordinating lime-green chair. Lara's Couch Potato doll lay near her, stuck between the sofa pillows. The living room furniture had belonged to Nikki's parents, had been given to her when they'd moved to Florida five years ago. That was one good thing about having elderly parents—you could get a houseful of furniture free. It was an odd mishmash of 1930s Art Deco hand-me-downs and the samples her parents had bought from her uncles Chris and Stavros, who'd been in the furniture-kit business. The room was pleasant and peaceful in spite of the fact that the circular pink mirror and frosted glass ashtray clashed with the handmade maple rocker and New England coffee table. None of it was beautiful or memorable, but Nikki had grown up with it. Each piece had special meaning.

She kicked off her shoes and put her feet on the coffee table, tried to read the paper. She kept coming back to Sunmann. Why would a loser like Sunmann have any contact with a winner like Douglas?

She tried to unwind, used a self-hypnosis technique that focused on slow, steady breathing, spent a few minutes in meditation, but was unable to distract herself. Let it go, she told herself. Tomorrow she'd talk to Douglas's widow, explore the connection. Tonight there was nothing to do except relax. So why couldn't she?

She left her tea in the living room, shuffled down the hall to Lara's room. Her niece was supposed to be asleep, but most nights when Nikki worked late she'd be awake, waiting for Nikki to come in and check on her.

She was sitting in bed, big-eyed, a quilt around the thin bump of her knees.

"Hi, honey. How come you're not asleep?"

"I don't know. I tried—I thought of all the things you told me. I counted ships and fish and cops, but nothing worked."

Like aunt, like niece. Nikki lifted the blanket and the girl slid under, lay flat. She tucked her in, spread the soft mass of curls. They lay like a loose shower of gold. Her glance was caught by an orange and black card on the floor. She picked it up, flipped it open. "What's this? Hey—you got invited to a Halloween party."

"I know. It's a kid who lives on the next block. But I'm not going."

"How come?"

Lara shrugged. "It's on Saturday."

Nikki understood. Saturday was Nikki's day off. When she was home Lara followed her around the house like a puppy. It would be good for Lara to be with kids her own age. She was tempted to push her to go but remembered what the guidance counselor had said. When Lara was ready she wouldn't need pushing. "But when will that be?" she'd asked the counselor.

"In her own time. She's still looking backward, missing her mother. You never know what'll help a kid, and let her get on with life."

Nikki bent now, picked up the invitation, and placed it on the dresser. "I brought you something." She went into the living room, came back with the schooner. Light from the hallway picked out its bronze sails.

"It's beautiful!"

"I'm going to put it up here," Nikki said, placing the statue next to the ship models her father had sent from Florida. She walked to the door. "Good night, honey."

"Aunt Nikki, can you read to me? We were in the middle of Cupid and Psyche."

"No, doll, it's late. You have school tomorrow—try to sleep."

"I can't." She paused. "I'm scared." Her voice was so low Nikki could hardly hear.

"What of?"

"I—I don't know."

This was as far as they ever got. Either Lara didn't know what she was afraid of or she didn't want to tell Nikki. There was a long silence while Nikki waited.

"I love you, Lara," she finally said.

"Mommy used to say that but then she went away."

Nikki felt as though a pair of hands had grabbed her throat; she couldn't breathe. "Mommy was very sick. She *had* to leave you. I'm not sick—I feel fine." Just bone tired and pulled in too many directions. "I won't leave you."

She sat on the edge of the bed, stroked the silky ringlets. "I'll stay here awhile. Close your eyes."

She'd wanted to hear what Lara was afraid of, but when she had, it had been almost too painful. But it was probably good for Lara to get it out.

After a while Nikki heard her deep, regular breathing. She tiptoed out of the room.

9

Nikki was crowded into a corner of the autopsy room, directly opposite the basin that held Frankie Sunmann's intestines. She'd once thought of becoming a surgeon but had never been able to stand clinical smells or the idea of cutting coldly into flesh and cartilage. Somehow the occasional gore of police work disturbed her less.

Pete Sunmann had ID'd the body. He'd left an hour ago, just before the autopsy started. Nikki had been fighting nausea since then, trying to find a safe place to look. If she took her eyes off the basin, she had several choices. She could watch Dr. Lonny Chi continue to cut what remained of Sunmann's body, weigh the organs, measure, speak into the overhead microphone as he dictated his report, or she could look at the floor under the metal gurney, spotted with blood like the back room of the butcher store where her mother had taken her to buy meat when she was little. She decided to look at the identification tag on Sunmann's right toe, marked with a "168," the number of the precinct where the case had originated.

One place she was careful not to look was directly to her right, where Det. Dave Lawton stood. She was sharply aware of his presence, as if the air between them were filled with signals. He'd done a quick but thorough inspection of her this morning, checked the length of her suit, the fit of her jacket. She'd dressed with special care, navy suit over a lime green blouse, telling herself it was important for her professional image and had nothing to do with him. Yet when she saw his appreciative glance, she had to admit she was pleased in spite of herself.

"All three slugs," he said to the doctor now, as Chi pulled the third bullet from the body with a pair of long tweezers. "How do you like that." She hated the fact that he was so relaxed, exchanging a joke every now and then with Chi, unperturbed by the scissoring, probing, mutilation of the body. As a homicide specialist Lawton had seen hundreds of autopsies. Her precinct work exposed her to few; in fact last year's *Times* had reported that the 168 was one of the few precincts in Brooklyn where violent crime was decreasing. A "country-club" precinct. She envied Lawton's poise. How could he be so cool while she kept tasting her breakfast?

"Looks like a slug from a thirty-eight," she said.

"Maybe." Lawton kept his eyes on Chi's hands. "You won't know for sure till Ballistics gets it."

Chi put the third bullet into a labeled plastic bag, continued his exploration of the body. She let her eyes wander over the nearby table where his assistant had laid out Sunmann's clothing as it was cut from the body. Samplings of the mud from his shoes had already been taken and were among the stack of plastic bags labeled for analysis.

Chi adjusted the microphone. "Meal last eaten appears to be white rice, pork, some liquid . . ."

"Chinese," Lawton said. "He didn't get it at the diner."

"He must've eaten it later than that," Nikki said. "They close at four-thirty."

The remaining minutes of the autopsy seemed to stretch

for hours. She spent the time looking at Lawton's gray suit, the loose, full jacket, the figured tie. What had *this* outfit cost? She realized she'd never seen him in the same clothes twice. Even when she'd met him at Coney Island—had that been the same shirt he'd worn in the morning? She didn't think so; somehow he'd managed to change in the middle of the day.

Lawton waited till Chi peeled off his rubber gloves and then asked, "What's your reading, doc, struggle or no struggle?"

Chi pushed his glasses up the bridge of his nose with a knuckle. "No fight as far as I can see. Nothing much under the nails. Dirt, the regular stuff you'd expect. But nothing that shouldn't be there. The lab'll test it out, but that's my gut feeling." He pointed to the track of the first stomach wound. "He wasn't even trying to run, from the way the bullet hit. Took it square—head-on."

Later, as Nikki and Lawton pushed past white-coated personnel in the lobby of the old medical building on Thirty-fourth Street, she remarked, "It was almost as though he was expecting something else, not a bullet."

Lawton nodded. "A handshake, maybe."

"Or a payoff."

"Drugs. Maybe he was pushing."

"Maybe," she said. "But he wasn't a junkie—at least no needle marks, no drugs in his system." She swerved to avoid an aide pushing a gurney. "His brother said he had a drug problem but he gave it up."

"Maybe his brother doesn't know."

"I found three joints in his room but that doesn't make him a druggie."

He held the plate glass door for her. "Got to keep digging."

Out on the street she thought of the piece of paper

with Barry Douglas's number on it that had been found in Sunmann's pocket. She hadn't had time to tell Lawton about that this morning, to bring him up-to-date. "You busy right now?" she asked. "Want to have something—coffee, maybe?"

"Best proposition today."

She hated being teased while she was working. A slow flush of annoyance spread upward from her throat.

"I should play hard to get, lady, but I'm destroyed by the color of your blouse."

She looked down at the lime green silk. "What's wrong?"

"Wrong? It couldn't be more right. Your eyes, Stretch—they look so blue. The green does it."

She hadn't been called "Stretch" since high school. "Listen, Lawton—" She stopped in mid-sentence, fighting an impulse to laugh. His teasing wasn't offensive, it was funny. But though the banter didn't mean anything, it was still unprofessional. "I hate personal remarks when I work," she said. "You wouldn't talk to a male cop that way."

"He wouldn't look like that in the blouse."

Sharp article. Was he always that quick? She turned away so he wouldn't see her smile.

They went to a greasy spoon on First Avenue. Lawton ordered black coffee, Nikki apple cinnamon tea. He backed away as the aroma hit him. "How do you drink that stuff?"

"It's pretty good. Try it."

"Are you kidding? I'll stick to the caffeine."

She told him about the report on the phone number in Sunmann's possession, showed him the articles on Douglas she'd clipped from the paper. He read them carefully.

" 'Wall Street wizard.' Hey I remember his name—the guy was in the papers four, five years ago, some kind of trouble with the Feds."

"Taxes?"

"No, wheeling and dealing. Penny stocks, if I remember right. But he weaseled out of it smelling like a rose, and then he and this other guy started a new firm." He paused for a moment, cup poised in midair. "Roth—that was his name. Roger Roth. What would Sunmann want with a guy like Douglas?"

"That's what I've been wondering."

"It couldn't have been business," he said. "Sunmann didn't have a pot to piss in."

"Maybe they were doing some kind of deal."

"Working together?" He raised his eyebrow, the triangular peak shooting up sharply. "I doubt it. His brother said Sunmann wasn't very big on work." He lifted his coffee. His hands were large, his fingers blunt; workman's hands.

"Sunmann had *something* cooking," she pointed out. "Remember what his friend Greenberg said—Sunmann told him if it worked out, he was going to buy a Ferrari."

"Yeah, something turned him on." He took gulps of the steaming coffee. "It bothers me. This guy Douglas is blown to bits on Sunday, and the next day Sunmann's killed."

"So?"

"It's coincidence. The guy who trained me told me never to believe in it."

She put away the clippings. "It's possible they *weren't* connected."

"My gut tells me they were."

"I thought I'd go see Douglas's widow, talk to her."

He picked up the check, let her lay down the tip. "And we can backtrack," he said. "Go see Sunmann's friend Arnold again, Lumberman, the landlord. See if anyone heard of Douglas, find out what they know."

They walked out on the street. Lawton had some paperwork waiting in his office. "Give me a call," he said. "I have some free time later—tell me where you'll be."

She was almost out of hearing, yards away, when he yelled across the crowded pavement, "Hey, Stretch—don't change the blouse."

Damn him! She dived around the corner toward the Fury, annoyed by the confusion she felt. Out of nowhere a funny thought crossed her mind, made her grin as she scrunched down into the car; if a blouse turned him on this way, what would a lime green nightgown do—make him pop out of his skin? *Why, Nikki,* she heard her grandmother's and mother's voices scolding her, echoes of an old-fashioned upbringing, *where did* that *thought come from?*

Manhattan Beach had its share of mansions, elegant homes tucked inside the quiet green blocks, far from city noises. It was funny seeing them from the other side of Sheepshead Bay. Nikki remembered passing them on her father's boat, pretending they were castles she'd read about in books, places royalty lived in.

They all tended to be large, but Douglas had lived in one of the biggest, a Greek revival building standing on half a block of lawn; white columns, brass knocker, antique lamp hanging in the doorway. Tara transplanted to Brooklyn. Carefully tended grass, clustered bushes, flower beds. Enough to keep a full-time gardener busy. A split-wood fence bordered the property on either side, left it open toward the street.

She walked up the path between two giant willows that brooded over the lawn, wondered what the house was worth, how much Douglas's heirs would inherit. How much insurance would they get in addition?

She rapped the brass knocker. A female voice asked through an intercom box, "Who is it?"

"Detective Trakos. Police."

The door was opened by a maid wearing a black uniform with a neat white collar and cuffs.

"Mrs. Douglas, please."

"Mrs. Douglas isn't here right now."

Through the space left by the open door Nikki had a clear view of the entry. It was awesome, two stories high. The floors and curved staircase were marble. A crystal chandelier hung overhead, sparkled with a thousand pieces of glass. The oils on the wall were originals, the Persian rug expensive.

The balcony of the second floor jutted toward the chandelier. A girl stood at the rail, dark hair like a billowing cloud, eyes red rimmed.

Nikki looked back at the maid. "When will Mrs. Douglas be here?"

"Not for a while."

"Is there anyone else I can talk to?"

The girl on the balcony said, "I'll handle it."

The maid thanked her and left while she came down the marble steps. She was young—not yet twenty—trying to act confident while her eyes gave her away. They were large and brown, luminous against pearly skin, full of hurt and anger. "Can I help you?" she asked.

Nikki fished out her badge. "Detective Trakos of the One Six Eight."

Something quickened behind the girl's glance, a sudden interest. "I'm Denise Douglas. Come in." Nikki remembered her name from the obituary—Douglas's daughter by a previous marriage.

She followed the girl into a sunlit lounge off the entry, comfortably furnished with wicker furniture, striped chintz cushions, and lots of throw pillows. Near a crowd of potted plants in the corner stood several cellophane-wrapped gift baskets stuffed with fruit and ribboned with mourning purple.

Denise peeked carefully through the sheer curtains that faced the front entry, then walked across to the sofa opposite the window. She motioned Nikki to a chair. Something about the tilt of her head and the proud classic features made Nikki think of pictures of young medieval noblewomen, protected and pure.

"My stepmother won't be back for hours." Her slim figure looked good in a taupe silk blouse and wool skirt. Deceptively simple clothes. The blouse alone would set Nikki back a month's rent. "My father was killed a few days ago," she explained in a low voice. "She went to set things up for the memorial service."

Nikki wondered why Denise hadn't gone, too. "I heard about the accident," she said. "I'm sorry."

"Thank you." For a minute Nikki thought she might add something, but she seemed to change her mind.

"Miss Douglas," Nikki asked, "does the name Francis Sunmann mean anything to you?"

She frowned. "No."

"Maybe you knew him as Frankie." Nikki took out the picture Pete Sunmann had given her, showed it to Denise.

The girl's soft hair rippled as she shook her head. "Why are you asking about him?"

"He was killed Monday night."

"How?"

"Shot to death."

"Ooh." The breath escaped from her slowly. Her mouth looked like a soft, rosy fruit.

"He had this address and phone number in his pocket," Nikki said.

"I'm sorry. I wish I could help you. I never saw him before."

Nikki started to rise.

"Detective Trakos . . . please stay a minute. Maybe your coming here was a godsend."

"What do you mean?"

"I don't know if you can help me, but if you can't"—she bit her lip—"you can tell me who to talk to."

Nikki sat down again, watched the girl run narrow, pale fingers through her hair.

"What do you know about my father's accident?" Denise asked.

"I saw it on the news. He had engine trouble—"

"He was *supposed* to have engine trouble." Her voice rose, wavered. "Someone set my father up—he was murdered."

Wait a *minute*, Nikki felt like saying. Everything seemed suddenly out of focus. From somewhere inside the house a clock chimed—strange, muted sounds. Denise was young for the shock of a death like her father's. Maybe her grief had converted itself into this peculiar frame of mind.

"I don't want you to think I gave a damn about him! We never had much of a relationship. I just don't want Arden to get away with it." Arden, Nikki remembered, was her stepmother's name. For a minute she wondered if Denise Douglas were temporarily unhinged. In a quiet, controlled way.

"It's a serious charge to call someone a murderer," Nikki said.

"You think I'm having a spell of the crazies, don't you?" Denise fought to keep emotion out of her voice. "My boyfriend told me this would happen if I tried to tell anyone. But I guess—I thought maybe you'd listen to me."

Nikki wondered what Denise's suspicions had to do with Sunmann's murder—if anything—and what she was getting into. Sunmann had to fit in here somehow, else why had Douglas's phone number and address been in his pocket when he'd died? "I'll listen. I don't know how much I can help you."

The girl's glance fled to the window again, then back. "I wasn't supposed to be here the night of the accident.

I'm a music major at Pardwick, upstate. But I wasn't feeling well. Strep throat. A bad one, I've still got it. The nurse thought I should see my own doctor, so I came home." She glanced down. "I don't know why I call this place home—I never come here. I—my parents were divorced. Up to six months ago I lived with my grandmother, but she died. If my boyfriend had his own apartment, I'd've gone there."

"Where's your mother?" Nikki asked.

"Someplace in Mexico, working on her suntan. We haven't talked in a couple of years." One hand pulled nervously at the fingers of the other. "I mean, I know my mother isn't much—I don't blame my father for leaving her. But Arden's a snake." Her mouth twisted to the side. "He thought she was a princess. If she sneezed, he'd run for a tissue. And look what she did to him."

A mischievous gleam showed in her eye, made her seem younger. "Arden damned near died when I walked in Sunday night. She had it all set up. She's very organized, used to be a nurse. That's how they met." The thick, dark hair fell over her shoulder, caught the light. "She couldn't sit still. She tried to watch TV, but she kept popping up to get things. Like she expected something to happen. And that was *before* the call came in from the Coast Guard."

"You were here when they called?"

She nodded. "When the guys came in from the Harbor Police, she put on a terrific act. 'Oh my God! My Barry!' " Denise rolled her eyes in imitation. "She's some actress. But *she knew* before they told her. Don't ask me how, but she knew—"

"It could have been real. She must have cared for your father—"

"Not really. That same night, the night her husband

blows into a million pieces, sweet Arden is on the phone with someone. 'Well, it's done,' she says."

"You listened in on the conversation?"

Her pale cheeks flushed. "The guest room—it's on the second floor, right above the den. I was lying down when I heard the phone ring downstairs. I found out you can hear noises through the floor; they come up along the heat pipe. I couldn't make out every word, but some of it was clear. She told him about me—"

"Him? How do you know it was a man?"

"I'll get to that in a minute. She told him, 'She's here, and there's nothing we can do now.' "

Denise looked anxiously at the window again. "She was talking to her lover. You'd have to know Arden to understand. There's always been a man in her life. If she planned to get rid of my father, she'd make sure there was someone lined up." She leaned forward, a winglet of hair falling toward her temple. "Anyhow, the next day she went to see him. I followed her."

Nikki raised an eyebrow.

"Well, she was acting strange," Denise said. "The houseman was back, Ramon Garcia. He runs things, keeps the other servants in line. Sunday was his day off. Arden insisted on going shopping herself, even though Ramon was there. I don't know why, it struck me funny. I mean, Brian was sick—she and my father had this kid three years ago. Arden was frantic about him. She lives for that kid—the sun rises and sets on his head. She keeps all kinds of medicine in the house, and she told me she would have given him something on her own. But she was worried enough to call the doctor. So here she is with a sick kid, her husband had just died the night before, and she runs out. It made me think about what I'd heard on the phone. So I sneaked down to my car and followed her. She went to a motel."

"Which one?"

"The Star Garden."

Nikki's stomach rippled. The motel the waitress had pointed out through the diner window yesterday morning, within walking distance of where Sunmann's body had been found.

"She went into one of the rooms, seemed to know exactly where she was headed. I couldn't see who opened the door. I hung around the office and when the kid on the desk walked away for a minute I got a look at the registration for that room. Mr. and Mrs. Amos Johnson."

"Okay, so she's having an affair. You may not like it, but it's not illegal."

"Killing my father is."

"Sure, but you need proof."

Her hands twisted together. "She's in a terrific hurry to be finished with my father, have it all over and done with. The memorial service is today at four-thirty. There's nothing to bury—I asked her why didn't she wait." She swallowed. "Maybe something would wash ashore. I mean, if it wasn't his whole body . . ." She let the sentence drift off, pain twisting her face. "But she said it was dumb to think that way. There was no hope they'd be able to identify anything. We should just go ahead and get it done."

"I'd like to attend the service." She'd call Lawton and tell him to meet her there. "It'll give me a chance to talk to your stepmother. Where is it?"

"Parkway Unitarian Center, in Bay Ridge."

The girl's glance suddenly darted to the window. She jumped to her feet.

Nikki turned. A tall young man was barreling up the front path toward the door. He was built like a bull, thick necked and muscular. His mouth clamped down in a straight line.

"Detective Trakos, please don't tell him what I said." She touched Nikki's hand, her fingers icy. "It's Rick, my boyfriend. If he knew I'd been talking to you—"

The knocker sounded. "*Please*—and when you talk to my stepmother, don't say that I—" The knocker banged again. "Thanks," she whispered, and ran to the entry.

Nikki heard her open the door.

"You ready?" the young man said. He sounded impatient.

"In a minute. All I have to do is change."

"Now? What the hell you been doing all this time? I thought I said—"

"Rick, *please*. A police officer's here. I've been talking to her."

"A cop? Why'd you—"

"Shh! Please."

They stepped into the doorway. Denise's smile was forced. "Rick Kerrigan, this is Detective Trakos."

He wasn't much older than the girl, but he looked a lot more worn, as though he'd already fought some battles with the world. He was very good-looking, in an Irish, snub-nosed way. Tough blue eyes, ruddy face, uncompromising jaw.

Nikki took out Sunmann's photo. "I asked Ms. Douglas about this man, Frankie Sunmann." She showed him the picture. "Do you know him?"

His glance ran quickly over the picture. He shook his head. "What happened to the guy?"

"He was killed night before last."

"How?"

"Someone shot him."

He looked uninterested, walked to the sofa, and sat down, drumming on the wicker with thick fingers.

Denise looked at him nervously. "I'm sorry to rush you, Detective Trakos, but I have to change for the service."

Was she frightened that Nikki would give away what they'd talked about or worried about Kerrigan's impatience?

Nikki took their names and addresses. Denise gave Pardwick College as her home address, not her stepmother's house. Kerrigan lived in Bensonhurst, with his mother. When Nikki asked where he worked, he snapped, "What do you need that for?"

"Routine." Why the strong reaction?

He looked uncomfortable, muttered, "First Traders Bank, Maiden Lane."

In the financial district. She wondered what he did for the bank—certainly not public relations.

The girl walked her to the door.

"I'll see you later," Nikki said.

Relief showed plainly in Denise's face.

11

She checked her desk. The Communications Bureau had sent the information she'd requested—911 had received a call at 2354 on Monday, had referred it to the nearest precinct, the 124 in Queens. She dialed the 124, learned that Sector Henry had responded. Oliver, one of the officers who'd made up the Sector Henry team that night, was in the station.

He remembered the call. "It was this big fat guy—a real five-by-five." That sounded like Arnold Greenberg. "He had two other guys with him. They told me they worked in Coney Island—they were on their way home."

"What was wrong with the car?"

"It was dead. We tried to give them a jump, but it wasn't the battery. A Ford Mustang. They had to be towed off."

That gave Greenberg an alibi for the time of Sunmann's murder.

The results of the auto canvass were in. Three cars had been on the street where Sunmann had died, two of them stolen. At least they could be reported to the owners. The third belonged to a man who worked at the water pollution plant. He'd parked there just after the diner owner had called in the murder. He always came in about then, between seven and seven-fifteen; his story checked out.

She phoned her confidential informant, Sam "the

Professor" Magliulo, but he didn't answer. The Professor would know about the shylocks Sunmann had owed, or if he didn't, he'd find out. He was one of the best stoolies the precinct had.

Jameson's skin was gray. A box of Alka-Seltzer lay on his desk near a glass of water.

"You okay?" Nikki asked.

"I need a plunger, mon." He gave her a sick smile.

"Where's Eagle-Eye?"

"Out. Should be back any minute."

That moved her into action. If she stayed, Eagle-Eye would expect a progress report. Was this Day One of the three days he'd allowed her or Day Two? She'd spent most of yesterday morning at the crime scene. Was he going to figure yesterday as a full day of investigation? She wasn't sure she wanted to know.

She called Sunmann's friend, Arnold Greenberg, arranged to meet him the following night for a replay of his final hours with Sunmann.

She adjusted her holster to ease the pressure on her shoulder, slipped on her jacket. Some women on the job kept their guns in their purse. She wore hers. It was easy to lose a purse, forget it, or have it stolen. The *Patrol Guide* said to keep it on your person, and besides, she liked to have it handy.

"See you later," she said to Jameson. "Hope you feel better."

The Parkway Unitarian Center was medieval Gothic, concrete spires rising from the smooth green cushion on Ninety-fifth Street. The big spreading dogwood out front was already bare but the maple was still scattering yellow patches on the lawn.

It took Nikki a few minutes to find Lawton. He was

inside the central arch, watching her approach. He wore a belted leather coat that seemed to broaden his shoulders by a yard. His eyes were busy, alert, taking in her every movement. All of a sudden she'd forgotten how to walk, how to put one foot ahead of the other. She moved ahead, uncomfortably aware of his glance.

"You waiting long?" she asked as she climbed the broad staircase.

"A while." He tried to meet her eyes but she looked away. She wanted him to notice her, but when he did, it drove her crazy.

Inside, an usher in a three-piece suit approached them. "May I help you?" he whispered.

"The Douglas service?" Nikki said. "And do you have a pay phone?"

"Straight ahead to the elevator for the service. The pay phone is all the way back at the end of the floor."

When she couldn't pick Lara up at school, she tried to call her at home in the afternoon. This morning Lara had gone to school reluctantly. Nikki had spent an hour coaxing her to dress, to move along.

Lara answered the phone, her small voice eager.

"How was today?" Nikki asked.

"Okay."

"What'd you do at latchkey?" The latchkey program was an extra hour at school for children whose parents worked.

"I didn't go. I called Mrs. Binsey and told her to come and get me. My stomach hurt."

Lara suffered from stomachaches that came more frequently whenever Nikki was deeply involved in her work. Though her niece had been checked carefully, no physical cause could be found. She never had them on weekends, when Nikki was home, or on Nikki's days off.

"How do you feel now?"

"Better. Are you coming home?"

"I'm working late."

"What about bedtime?"

She felt a spasm of guilt. "I can't promise. Don't wait up. If I'm not there, I'll see you in the morning."

She hung up and frowned, aware of Lawton's glance.

"What's wrong?"

"My niece. I don't know how people raise big families—I only have one and I never seem to give her enough time."

"Cops' kids have to adjust. Mine did after a while."

Was he telling her she worried too much? This wasn't the time or place to go into a long discussion, but as they walked to the elevator she wondered what he'd meant. Had his kids "adjusted" because his wife had been alive then, available to care for them?

He pressed the elevator button. They crowded inside the tiny car with a tall, suntanned man, expensively dressed in a dark pinstripe, his silvery hair professionally combed. A slight frown drew his eyebrows together. He seemed anxious, or was it impatient? The pungent scent of musk filled Nikki's nostrils. The elevator rose slowly, discreetly. Its doors slid open on the second floor.

Some yards away a short, tawny-skinned man stood guard outside the chapel door, his hair smoothly slicked back, his eyes sharp. He came up to Nikki's collarbone; she had a clear view of his narrow, sleek head. He reminded her of a lemming.

He held a thin brown cigarillo in nicotine-stained fingers. "Book, pleess," he said with a pronounced Hispanic accent, pushing the leather-bound memoriam toward them. Fortyish, the kind of man you didn't fool with. Carried himself like a bantam-weight fighter.

The silver-haired man signed the book, "Roger Roth," with a bold flourish. Douglas's partner. He pushed open the oak door, went inside.

Nikki and Lawton tried to follow but the lemming intercepted them. "Book, pleess."

"We're not really guests," she said.

"Pleess, book," the man insisted. His expression was serious. "No speak Inglés."

Lawton flipped open his badge case. "We're police."

The man's face registered surprise. His eyes narrowed. "Who you want?"

"Mrs. Douglas," Lawton said. "We'll wait inside till we can talk to her." Lawton tried to put his palm on the door but the lemming stood in his way, his mouth tight.

"No," he said flatly. "Iss private. Family."

"Listen, mister," Lawton said, "you have a choice—either we go in quietly or noisily. Your English is good enough for that, isn't it?"

The man's eyes calculated; his jaw hardened.

The muscle had begun to work in Lawton's cheek again. "You don't want to mess up our police work with your little games, do you?"

He treated Lawton to a blistering look. Lawton moved his hand to the door.

Nikki took a step forward, said softly, "It's so hard when there's been a death in the family." The small man looked at her, made a noise deep in his throat that sounded like a grunt. His eyes shifted, looked dangerous. "I'm sure you're just doing your job."

"Mees Douglas, she say private."

She gave him what she hoped was her most engaging smile. "I'm sure she won't mind—just for a *few* minutes."

His glance slid away. He stepped aside.

"Thanks *very* much."

They pushed past. Lawton asked the man, "What'd you say your name was?"

"Ramon Garcia."

"I'll remember that."

When they were out of earshot Nikki whispered, "That's the houseman Denise mentioned. I don't think you made a friend."

"Tough. They don't pay us to make friends."

The chapel was a shallow bowl, the outer rings of seats slightly higher than the center, which held a raised pulpit. A hidden organ played a hymn. The benches were filled, about fifty people in all. A scattering of minks, the flash of expensive jewelry, the modulated buzz of polite whispers.

Nikki and Lawton took seats at the back, in the outermost ring. Kerrigan and Denise were sitting at the end of a row, off by themselves. The girl still wore the taupe blouse but had changed to a black suit. "There's Douglas's daughter with her boyfriend," Nikki whispered. "The pretty girl with the dark hair. I wonder where her stepmother is."

"Probably the one our little friend is headed for," he answered, tilting his head toward the opposite aisle. Ramon Garcia had hurried in and zipped down front toward a slim, red-haired woman in a black dress who sat near the pulpit next to Roth, Douglas's business partner. "My money's on her," Lawton said. "Watch."

Garcia said something in her ear, and the woman turned to look. Her large green eyes searched till she found them. Bright auburn curls framed her features, made her memorable. Her skin had been tanned in outdoor play, Nikki guessed, not a farmer's tan but a sunbather's. She looked intelligent, practical, and direct. She caught Nikki staring and looked away.

The minister, a woman in her early thirties, entered the pulpit. Garcia slunk toward the exit, and the service began.

The minister spoke movingly about a celebration of Barry Douglas's life. He had been a family man, had provided well for his wife and children. Indeed, he had many accomplishments in the business world his survivors could point to with pride. Roger Roth's mouth twisted sourly; he squirmed in his seat. Douglas was mourned, the minister went on. He would be missed. She hoped his soul would rest in eternal peace.

The organ played, prayers were read. It wasn't like a Greek Orthodox funeral where the women wept and the priest chanted. Denise was the only one who showed any feeling. Although the girl had said her father meant nothing to her, she wiped her eyes with a tissue, gripped Kerrigan's hand till her knuckles were white. Otherwise there was a coolness here, an emotional distance. There seemed to be a thought just beyond that one, teasing Nikki with its importance. She looked at the red-haired woman. Her eyes were on the minister; she seemed intent on every word. Nikki couldn't figure out why she felt troubled. If she could, she might have an important piece of information.

After the service, people gravitated toward the redhead. They held her hand briefly, murmured a few words, then left in twos and threes. Arden Douglas handled the scene with cool, gracious competence. Denise said nothing to her stepmother. She gave Nikki a sidelong glance as she left; Kerrigan hardly looked at them.

As the chapel emptied, Lawton and Nikki stood up. Arden Douglas was talking to Roth, Douglas's partner, the only remaining guest. He seemed agitated, pointed something out in a heated whisper, gesturing impatiently. Nikki overheard him say, ". . . lay off half the staff."

"I don't know what I can do about that, Roger," Arden said. "Look, why don't you go on to the house, and we can talk about it there."

He turned and glared at Nikki and Lawton. His eyes, under a deeply creased forehead, were vividly blue and full of trouble. The oak doors swung on their hinges as he left.

Arden Douglas looked up at Nikki and Lawton as they walked toward her. Nikki whispered, "Let me have this one," heard Lawton agree in a low murmur.

Douglas's widow was a striking woman, Nikki decided. Not too many looked that good when you were next to them. A few stray freckles showed on her smooth skin, fit in with her casual, easy air. Her hair was a bright accent, natural looking and shining. It was hard to judge her age—somewhere over thirty and under forty. Everything she wore looked like Madison Avenue, the stylishly draped dress, the rope of pearls, the thick gold bracelet. Even her voice was rich, deep and cultivated. "I'm Arden Douglas. Ramon told me you were from the police."

"Detective Trakos of the One Six Eight," Nikki said. "Sorry to bother you here, Mrs. Douglas. We have a few questions."

"That's all right. Whatever I can do to help. Although I don't know what else I can tell you. I've already spoken to the Harbor Police and the Coast Guard."

"This isn't about your husband's death."

Two slender fingers reached for the necklace, rotated a pearl. "What *is* it about?"

If she told her, Arden could deny knowing Francis Sunmann and send them on their way. For some reason Nikki didn't want that to happen. She wanted time with the widow. Was that because of what Denise had told her earlier? She wondered whether Arden's lover had been at the service. Or had he stayed away, afraid he might call attention to himself?

"It's going to take more than a few minutes," Nikki said.

Garcia called from the door, "Car, madam."

"I really have to go," Arden said. "Some friends are coming to the house—"

"Why don't we follow you? We'll wait till you find a little time."

She hesitated. "I guess it'll be okay. You may have to wait awhile."

"That's all right, Mrs. Douglas."

Sometimes she learned more just by absorbing the atmosphere of a place, looking around rather than asking questions.

When they were out on the street Lawton said, "A smooth piece."

"She seemed on the up and up."

"Those are the trickiest kind." He took out his car keys. "I have to go downtown."

"The duffel bag case?"

"Yeah. The wife's letting one of our guys take her to the boyfriend's funeral—she heard the place was going to get shot up."

"She's beginning to trust you."

"A little. It's a good sign." He folded his coat over his arm. "Talk to you later, over dinner. You can bring me up to date."

"Okay." How smoothly he'd worked the two together—after all, she had to give her partner a recap, didn't she? And some time during the evening she had to eat, too.

They arranged to meet at Johnny's Wok on Flatbush Avenue at six-thirty. Whoever came first would take a table and wait.

12

This time, Nikki didn't even have to lift the brass knocker on the door of the Douglas house. The door swung inward as she raised her hand.

Garcia glared up at her, feet slightly apart in a fighter's stance. His eyes had an ugly look. They made her remember a kid they'd picked up some years ago for loitering, who hadn't wanted to answer any questions. It turned out he'd just come from his mother's house, where he'd plunged a broken wine bottle into her armpit, left her to bleed to death. Garcia's eyes had the same crazy look.

He stepped aside so she could enter. A tub of long-stemmed white roses had been placed on the marble floor, under the chandelier. There must have been fifty flowers; they perfumed the air.

Directly ahead, from deep inside, came the sounds of ice against glasses, people talking. Garcia was careful to steer her quickly to the right, down a carpeted hall. "Thees way."

He showed her into a library done in shades of sand, mocha, and wood. "She say wait." He spoke to her right earlobe, avoiding her glance. He left her, his feet noiseless on the deep carpeting.

She crossed to the shelves of books, looked at the titles. Historical novels, thick volumes with shiny jackets. She flipped one open. No bookplate or name. Did they belong to Arden? Maybe she filled her lonely nights with reading—among other activities. How many other people lived in the house besides her? How many servants, for instance. Garcia? The maid who'd answered the door the first time she'd come? Or did Arden tie on a fresh apron every morning and clean the place herself?

She slid the book back on the shelf. A best-seller lay on the ledge under it, as though someone had been reading it and set it down for a moment. A sheet of paper was stuck in as a bookmark. It held a penciled list, the backsloping handwriting strong and even in its proportions. "Ice, crackers, cheese . . ." Someone planning a party. "Call minister, office, insurance comp—" An icy finger tickled her spine. Someone making a list for the memorial service.

Why did that give her the creeps? After all, someone had to deal with death and burial.

Then why did the list trouble her? It stuck in her head with other bits of information floating around unconnected, loose facts and images only half understood. Like memories of the widow at the chapel. What was it about the way she looked?

She pocketed the list and cruised along the shelves, looking at the book spines. At the end was a group of nursing texts. She lifted out *Modern Nursing Practice* and opened it. Inside the front cover it was signed "Arden Bittnauer" in the same backsloping handwriting. Denise had mentioned her stepmother had been a nurse.

She put the book back. A rectangle of color caught her eye, a red steno book propped against the side of a shelf. Only the first page was filled. "*Hablar*, to speak. *Amar*, to love, *dormir*, to sleep. The handwriting was different from the other samples she'd found, loose and slanting, large capitals, a hasty, fluid scrawl.

Someone learning English. There was a Spanish-English dictionary under the steno book.

Could be Garcia. But would he keep his stuff here? She put the two books back, wondered whether Garcia had the run of the place. She didn't like the look of the man. He was high on her list of people who might be involved in Sunmann's murder.

A sound made her turn. A little boy bounded into the room, announced cheerily, "Hi!" He was under three, friendly and outgoing, with eyes like huge black grapes. He rolled a toy car across the carpet, watched it collide with her shoe.

"Hey," Nikki said, "that's a moving violation."

"My name Brian," the boy said.

"Hello." Arden's son, the child she and Barry had had. He smiled craftily. "I see Poppy."

"Poppy?"

He nodded, pointed toward a silver-framed photo on the desk. The picture showed an older Barry Douglas than she'd seen in the newspaper. Deeply suntanned, heavyset, standing in front of his motorboat in a pair of bathing trunks, with a white yacht cap perched on the back of his head. His hairy, muscular chest bulged. He'd been somewhat overweight, even a little paunchy. The thick, dark hair had begun to recede from his forehead. Not a very good-looking man. Obviously not handsome enough to hold the attention of the captivating Arden, if she'd had to take a lover. What had attracted her in the first place? Not his physique. But maybe Arden had seen the bulge of his wallet—that might have given him just the right shape.

One of Douglas's large hands caressed the boat's rail. *Arden's Dream.* Nikki remembered the name from the papers. What was left of the *Dream* lay in splinters at the bottom of the bay.

"Poppy," Brian said proudly, pointing to the picture.

"I see him," she said.

"No." He shook his head, his underlip jutting out. He looked like a miniature of his father.

There was a whisper of noise in the doorway. Arden stood watching, tense and alert. How long had she been there? She straightened and caught Nikki's glance, put a serene look on her face.

She sailed in and scooped up her son. "Briny, what are you doing down here, baby?" She was smiling coolly now, the anxiety gone from her green eyes. "How long has he been here?"

"A few minutes," Nikki said.

"I hope he hasn't chewed your ear off." So that was it. What was she afraid the boy might say? Family secrets from the mouth of a three-year-old? "Once he starts, he's a real chatterbox. If you don't mind waiting just another minute, I'll get someone to take him, and then we can talk."

She was good, Nikki thought, watching her walk into the hall. If she hadn't seen the fear on Arden's face just minutes before she'd never have imagined it. She remembered Lawton's comment, *a smooth piece*.

"Ramon," Nikki heard her call.

While they waited, Brian said amiably, "Mommy, I talk to lady."

"Yes, baby."

Garcia appeared in the doorway, gave Nikki his tight-lipped stare.

"I want Brian to stay in his room—he has a cold," Arden told Garcia. "Get one of the girls to keep him company, and make sure he doesn't wander." She took a step into the hall and added something too low for Nikki to make out.

She came back, smoothing the sleeve of her black dress. A diamond the size of an egg caught the light. No doubt it had cost more than Nikki's Camaro.

Arden sank into the velvet cushions of the sofa, indicated a chair opposite. She seemed younger, more uncertain in that posture. "I haven't told Brian about his father yet. He's so little. I mean, how do you . . ." She lifted her shoulders helplessly.

"It must have been a shock," Nikki said.

"It was." She turned the ring with her thumb. "I'd just spoken to Barry on the phone—he had one of these ship-to-shore lines. He told me he was having trouble starting up and was going to call the Coast Guard." She rubbed her forehead with a mauve-tipped finger. "An hour later they brought me the news."

She seemed sad. Why not? Nikki thought. Having a lover didn't automatically mean she hated her husband. She could have cared about both men—some women did. And anyhow, who said she *did* have a lover? Nikki was only taking Denise's word for it. She felt suddenly uneasy—she would have to test Denise's murder theory on Arden. She hadn't promised the girl she'd keep quiet about it, and yet she was concerned about what might happen if she spoke. Would she put Denise in danger?

She pulled herself up short. She couldn't afford to think that way. As a cop her loyalty had to be to the truth, not to individuals. If Arden were challenged, she might let something slip, something that might crack the case open. She would wait for the right moment, plunge in.

"Was your husband an experienced sailor?" she asked.

"Oh, yes. I mean, he'd had a boat for twenty years, ever since he was a kid. He knew what he was doing."

"Maybe something went wrong mechanically."

"That's what they think. The boat was new—only two

years old. If it was defective, that company has a lot to answer for. I'm going to have them bring up the engine, so it can be tested."

She looked down at an issue of *Connoisseur* on the coffee table. "Of course ... there's another possibility. I hate to even think of it. I mean, Barry had been having problems at his firm—*real* problems. Maybe they got to be too much for him. . . ." For an instant she was lost in her thoughts. "I'm sorry. You didn't come here to listen to my troubles."

She tucked her legs under her, laid her hand on the chair arm. "I understand you spoke to my stepdaughter earlier."

Ah, here it was. "That's right."

"She's pretty upset."

Nikki took a deep breath, knowing what she had to do but uncomfortable with her decision. Denise, if she ever found out Nikki had repeated her story, wouldn't confide in her again. She'd be lost as a source of information.

Nikki watched Arden carefully to see the effect her words would have. "She told me a weird story. Claims there's another man in your life, that your husband's death was no accident."

Lines of disbelief and concern gathered at the corners of Arden's eyes. "I'm worried about her," she said. Nikki wanted to believe in her sincerity—what was it that stopped her?

"On Monday, the day after the explosion, she followed you to a motel—"

"A motel?"

"According to her, you slipped out to meet this man."

"That's crazy. Why would I go anywhere the day after Barry died? And Brian was sick—I'd called the doctor."

"That's what made her suspicious, that you'd leave after that."

She shook her head. "I don't know whether to talk to her about this or just wait and hope it'll pass. Maybe she needs a psychiatrist."

"She's having a hard time."

"That's obvious."

She'd milked Denise's story for all it was worth. She wasn't sure she'd gained anything by revealing it. "Mrs. Douglas, I came to see you about someone named Francis Sunmann. Sound familiar?"

"No. What did you say his name was?"

His name. Nikki hadn't said it was a him; Francis sounded like "Frances," could have been a female. "Sunmann. He was called Frankie."

Arden shook her head.

Nikki pulled out the photo and Arden studied it. "No one I ever saw. Why are you asking about him?"

"He was killed two nights ago, the day after your husband's accident."

She frowned, nodded. "Who was he, anyhow?"

Nikki noted that she hadn't asked how he was killed, the usual question. "A small-time gambler. Lived over in Bensonhurst."

"Oh." She stared at the picture. "What's the connection? Why are you coming to me?"

"He had your phone number in his pocket."

"Really? That's odd."

"And your address." Nikki took out a copy of the scribbled note that had been found on the body, laid it next to the photo. "We thought there might be some reason."

The frown deepened, drawing together two freckles near the top of her nose. She handed back the snapshot and the note.

"Maybe your husband knew him."

"Maybe."

"He could have been a business connection, someone from your husband's office."

Arden pulled a cigarette from an inlaid box on the coffee table, lit it with a lighter set into a marble ball. "He never mentioned the guy."

Nikki took out her memo book. "Can you give me your husband's business address?"

Arden went to the desk, came back with an embossed, cream-colored card: DOUGLAS, ROTH ASSOCIATES; BARRY DOUGLAS, PARTNER. A phone number was printed in the corner opposite a Water Street address—in the Wall Street area.

Nikki asked, "Any ideas on why Sunmann might have had this number?"

"No." She inhaled deeply, blew smoke from finely shaped nostrils. She glanced toward the door and Nikki became aware of the distant sound of people talking, drinking.

"Anything at all?" Nikki asked. "Even something small—"

"Well, the only thing . . . You know, right after Barry died, when the story was on the news, we did get some crazy calls. Cranks."

"What did they want?"

"One wanted to send me money if I needed it, another was looking for information for an article about the accident. Some guy wanted to meet me—junk like that."

"Did you report the calls?"

"No. I just figured if it went on . . ."

"Did anyone get their names?"

"No. But maybe this Sunmann was one of them. Why else would he have my number?" She bent and stubbed out her cigarette in a bronze ashtray shaped like a hand. She paused. "You know, I just had another thought. Maybe it wasn't *my* number at all. This man could have been connected with Denise or that crazy boyfriend of hers. He sounds like the type. There wasn't any name on the paper you showed me, was there?"

"No."

"That must be it. Barry was always worried about this Kerrigan character, what he'd do. Kerrigan was at Pardwick with Denise until they threw him out—he was in trouble up there."

"What kind of trouble?"

"Something to do with drugs. And he hurt someone—I'm not sure how. Barry didn't want Denise to stay with him after that but she wouldn't listen. He was afraid she'd get hurt."

Nikki made a note in her memo book. "I'll check on it, Mrs. Douglas, but it doesn't make sense. Why would your stepdaughter or her boyfriend tell Sunmann to contact them here? She told me she's hardly ever here—"

"I don't believe she said that. I think she wishes she didn't have to be here, but she does. It's sad. She has nowhere else to go. She spent her summer here, all her holidays so far. And each time she comes, that wild nut shows up with her." A guest laughed loudly, deep in the interior of the house. Arden stood, smoothed the dress around her hips.

Nikki rose, too. "Thanks for your time, Mrs. Douglas." Arden still hadn't asked how Sunmann had been killed. Maybe she already knew, Nikki speculated. "Before I go, I'd like to talk to Mr. Garcia."

"He's gone. This is his half-day."

He'd left suddenly, hadn't he? With a house overflowing with guests, wouldn't Arden need his help?

"He won't be in till tomorrow," Arden said.

"He lives here?"

"No, in the Bronx with a daughter."

"Could I have his address?"

"He just moved. I don't have it."

Nikki followed her toward the door, watched the rhythmic, seductive swing of her hips. She tried to picture Arden with her husband. Beauty with the beast.

"Someone'll show you out," Arden said, moving quickly along the hallway.

A minute later the black-uniformed maid who'd let her in earlier appeared. "This way, please."

Nikki followed her toward the door.

As she left she almost collided with a boy delivering a memorial basket. It made her think of Uncle Spyros's death. She walked down the flagstone path, remembering the days right after the funeral when his house had been full of fruit and flower baskets. She pictured Aunt Eleni, eyes red rimmed and sunk into her gray skin, wearing widow's black from head to toe, bursting now and then into a keening wail that pierced Nikki's heart. Suddenly she knew what had been bothering her about Arden. No one would ever convince Nikki that this widow was grieving. It wasn't a matter of style but of substance.

She thought about the pieces that didn't fit. Arden had sat coolly in the library and read a best-seller while she'd made out a list of details for the memorial service. At the chapel she'd been competent and gracious. Where were the tears—or the stiffness of swallowed grief? She was good, but not that good. She didn't make it seem real.

13

Lawton dipped his chopsticks into the bowl of bean curd soup, fished up a straw mushroom. "So what'd you find out?"

"I'm not sure," Nikki said. "I don't even know who Sunmann wanted in the Douglas place. Could be Douglas, his widow, or even the daughter or her boyfriend." She flipped open her napkin, spread it on her lap. "Something funny's going on. The daughter says she hardly ever comes home; the stepmother says she's there all the time. I'm going to call the girl's school tomorrow, see what I can find out." She spooned up some soup, crunched on a snowpea. "The boyfriend's got a short fuse. The girl looks scared out of her wits whenever he's around. The stepmother says he's been mixed up with drugs, that he was thrown out of school because he hurt someone—she doesn't know exactly how."

Lawton lifted his eyebrow. "The boyfriend's a little young to be Sunmann's buddy."

"Not if they were in some deal together."

"Did you get to talk to the little guy?"

"Garcia?"

"Yeah."

"No. He left early."

"Good. I want to be there." He took a piece of paper

and the stub of a pencil from his pocket, made a note. "I'll check him out tomorrow." She noted his eagerness, remembered how Garcia had irritated him at the memorial service.

He poured tea, left the pot uncovered to show the waiter they needed a refill. He'd shaved since this afternoon and changed his shirt to a subtly striped blend. The brown stripe matched the color of his eyes. Toward the center of each iris shimmering bits of darker color floated. They intensified his expression, made him seem amused. She found herself noticing how black they were, like tiny pieces of obsidian. She became annoyed with herself. It was the third or fourth time during the meal her concentration had slipped from the case.

She forced herself back to the murder. "One thing struck me funny," she said. "Denise followed her stepmother to a motel the day Sunmann died—"

"Or she says she did."

"It's the Star Garden—right near where Sunmann got it."

"What happened at the motel?"

"Arden met her lover, according to Denise. She got a look at the register—they'd signed in as Mr. and Mrs. Amos Johnson."

"A phony if I ever heard one," he said. "Smith, Johnson—they top my list of favorite phonies. You check it out yet?"

"No, I just got it."

The waiter brought his sha-cha chicken in a bird's nest. She ate her lo mein, admired the way Lawton lifted mouthfuls of braided noodle so adeptly with his chopsticks. She'd never been able to use them.

She tipped her fork with mustard, dipped it into the lo mein. "Want to go to the motel tonight?"

"Stretch, you keep surprising me."

"Very funny. I meant the Star Garden."

"Hey, you can't blame me for trying."

She kept her eyes on the food, concentrated on chewing. "Maybe someone over there saw Sunmann or this Amos Johnson."

"Okay, why not."

He signaled for the check. Nikki asked, "How's your other case?"

"Good. The wife gave us his gun."

"The duffel bag guy?"

"Yeah. It means we can make him in some of the open cases we got, but more than that, it shows she's beginning to get cozy."

"She'll talk?"

"Soon."

The waiter brought the check, tucked into a dish of orange slices and fortune cookies.

Lawton lifted a cookie, took out a slip of paper. "Terrific! 'Your current enterprise will meet with success.' That means we'll find the guy that did Sunmann, with the gun tucked in his pocket nice and neat so we can take him into court."

She reached for a cookie, felt his eyes on her as she opened it.

"What does yours say?" he asked.

"That's funny—the same thing."

She took a quick look at the paper in her palm before she crushed it. It read, "Don't turn away from the new romance in your life." She tucked the crumpled slip into her pocket.

Sid Bender, manager of the Star Garden Motel, was short and dark, with a pencil-thin mustache and a fussy habit of rubbing the tips of his fingers together. When the boy at the desk called into the back room that police were there to see him, Bender came out scowling. "You don't have to announce it to the world," he told the clerk.

He led Nikki and Lawton into the back, showed them chairs next to a dusty artificial corn plant. A ceramic fisherman sat on the edge of the pot, trolling the soil. "That kid has air where his brains should be, yelling out loud that the cops want to see me. How good can that be for business?"

She could see why he was worried. Except for the clerk, the lobby had been empty. In fact the whole place had a bypassed, run-down look. Only three cars had been parked in the lot, in a space that would have accommodated thirty.

"What can I do for you?" Bender said to her, steepling his fingers and leaning forward. His smile was flirtatious. What was it about men with narrow mustaches—they all wanted to be lovers. This one was small enough to sit in her lap, though she had no urge to put him there.

Lawton laid Sunmann's photo on the desk. "Ever see this man?"

Bender shook his head. "Not that I remember."

"How about your clerk?"

He called "Kevin!" and then smoothed his mustache with a swipe of his finger while they waited.

The kid shuffled in, looking bored, his sandy hair falling in stiff peaks over his eyes. Lawton pointed to the photo, asked if he recognized the face. "Never saw the guy."

Lawton turned back to Bender. "How about a man named Amos Johnson?" he asked Bender. "Stayed here around the thirteenth, fourteenth."

"Let's see." His mustache wriggled. "Kevin," he said,

"go get the book." He said casually to Nikki, "It's hard to remember everyone who stays here."

She'd heard enough about the motel to realize he was living in fantasyland. Maybe he thought if he kept wishing the Star Garden was a thriving establishment instead of the little hole in the wall it was, that would make it happen. It was too far from Kennedy Airport to compete with the Hilton or Marriott, too seedy looking; it thrived on fast turnovers by couples needing privacy. An overnight guest was an event.

Kevin came back with a big book, dumped it unceremoniously on Bender's desk. Bender gave him a withering look, then flipped through the fingerworn pages. "Here it is, 'Mr. and Mrs. Amos Johnson, 27500 Moss Lane, Canton, Ohio.' No zip." Nikki copied the address into her memo book, wondered if it would turn out to be a phony. The handwriting was unfamiliar, a neat slant, unlike either sample she'd found in the Douglas library.

"Car license?" Lawton asked.

Bender looked again, then pursed his lips tightly and glared at the clerk. "Kevin, you didn't get the number."

The kid squinted at the book, then shrugged. "Forgot."

Bender looked disgusted. "At any rate they took the room for three nights, from the twelfth through the fourteenth—"

"Yeah," Kevin put in, "but they only stayed one."

Lawton asked, "How do you know?"

"Chambermaid told me. She went in the day they took the room and it wasn't used. Just the one suitcase in the closet."

"Locked?"

"Yeah." He reddened. It was an admission that he'd tried to open it.

Lawton said, "That was the twelfth." Two days before Sunmann was killed.

"Yeah. And the next night they slept there, but they didn't want the room cleaned. He called at night—musta been ten, eleven—and said he wanted to sleep late the next day and not to send the chambermaid in, he'd manage by himself."

Bender explained, "She cleans in the morning."

"Did they have any visitors?"

"Nope." Kevin yawned, showing irregular yellow teeth.

"So the only time you saw him was when he registered," Lawton said.

He shook his head. "*She* registered. He was outside. In the car, I guess."

Lawton asked, "What'd she look like?"

"Real good." A lopsided grin filled his face. "A real sharp-looking piece." He looked at Nikki apologetically. "She had a lot of dark, curly hair, like Brooke Shields, except maybe a little older."

"How much?"

"I couldn't even guess. She had on these big sunglasses, even when she was signing the book, so I couldn't see a lot of her face."

"She use a credit card?"

"No, cash." Somehow Nikki had anticipated that. "Oh, before that, she wants to see the room. I say, okay, I'll show you. But she says just give her the key, she'll find it. If her husband and her like it, they'll take it. Which they did."

"You saw the husband, too?"

"Not then. Only once, just before they left. Musta been midnight or a little before—"

"On the fourteenth—"

"That's right."

The night Sunmann was killed.

"It suddenly turns nasty and starts to rain. I'm shutting the windows in the back when I see him come out of his room alone. Funny time to be marching around in this neighborhood, but I figure maybe the wife's hungry and the guy's going down to Sheepshead Bay for something. I'm waiting to hear the car start up, but I don't. Then I realize wherever he's going, he's walking. In the rain yet, but that's his business."

"They didn't have the car?"

"I didn't see it. I mean he wasn't in it, and I didn't see it in the lot." He tossed his head so the points of his hair fell around his ears. "So I'm watching the late show and sort of keeping an ear open for when he gets back. The funny thing is, he don't come back. After a while, I think maybe I'm wrong, and just to check, I go take a look. And his door's open. The place is empty. No wife, no suitcase, no car, no nothing. Never came back."

"Can you describe the guy?"

"Nope. It was dark, and all I could see was a guy in a coat. He wasn't too close, either."

"Fat, thin, tall . . . color of his hair, maybe?"

"No, too far away, and it was raining, too."

Lawton looked over at Nikki to see if she had any questions. "What did the car look like?" she asked.

"Tell you the truth, I never noticed."

He'd been too busy looking at the woman who'd registered.

"I'd like to see the room they stayed in," Nikki said.

"No problem," Bender said.

He led them to 31 on the second floor of the two-story structure.

There was nothing much to see. The drawers and closets were empty, the wastebaskets fitted with new plastic liners.

"It was cleaned after they left?" she asked Bender.

"Oh yes, twice." He smoothed his mustache with the back of a knuckle. "In fact, it was rented to another party yesterday."

The mirrors and bureau tops looked as though they'd been sprayed and wiped. Still, there'd be plenty of fingerprints, probably hundreds, considering all the people who'd used the room—too many to make it worthwhile to dust.

She wandered out to the walkway, a sort of balcony that ran around the upper level, turned to look in all directions, was suddenly caught by a familiar shape. She squinted, then recognized it.

There was the diner, clearly visible from where she stood.

14

"The room was taken by what the kid called a 'real sharp-looking piece,'" Nikki said to Lawton as they drove away from the station house in her Camaro. "But she had dark, curly hair—not auburn, like Arden's."

"She could've been wearing a wig and sunglasses."

"What about the handwriting? It's not like either sample I found in the house."

"That can be faked."

She eased onto Coney Island Avenue. A pale moon hid behind the clouds, peeked through in patches. "Why'd they take the place for three days, I wonder."

"That's a naive question."

"You know what I mean—they only used it one night."

He shrugged. "Who knows? The widow's cheating on Douglas with this guy in the motel, who's cheating on *her* with the curly-haired broad. Anyhow, what do all these jokers have to do with Sunmann?"

"I wish I knew. I get strong vibes about that guy running out of the motel the night Sunmann got it, never coming back."

"You think he's the perp?"

"I get a real gut feeling. The time matches pretty close, and he wasn't far—five blocks or so. There's something about the way they left; they ran."

"Or *he* did," Lawton said. "No one saw the curly-haired broad after she registered. Remember, the kid didn't see her come out."

She changed lanes to avoid a double-parked car. "Okay, what if she *was* Arden, all along? She could be home, waiting for his call."

"Now all we have to do is find the guy who was in the motel, figure out what his connection to Sunmann was, and prove it in court. A snap."

At Kings Highway she stopped for a light. The case nagged at her. "I wish to hell we knew who in Douglas's place Sunmann was connected with. I keep wondering whether we're going to spend all this time tracking down the Douglas lead, and end up at square one again."

"Those are the breaks. You have to look under every rock."

She turned into her street, drove beneath the old trees. She'd offered to take Lawton to his car, but he'd insisted on seeing her home safely; he would find a cab. She was aware of him in the enclosed space, had been aware of him all day. She didn't want to think about it. The last thing she needed right now was chemistry between her and her partner. Yet she was unable to come up with anything to fill the silence. She pulled under the maple that shadowed the driveway, heard the intense quiet as she shut the motor.

She turned toward him and started to say good night, but suddenly he was kissing her, his mouth rough but exciting. She let the kiss go on, then pulled back, breathless.

"I could use a cup of coffee," he whispered.

"I can't. I've got my niece upstairs—I told you about her."

"The kid doesn't let you have friends in?"

"Don't get cute. It's just she hasn't seen me all day."

"So let's go up, and she'll see you."

"I mean alone."

"Why does it have to be alone?"

"Because she needs that time with me, just the two of us together. Look, she's not an ordinary kid. I've had all kinds of sweat with her. Half the mornings I wake up I'm afraid she's going to say she doesn't want to go to school."

"So?"

"So I have to stand there and argue and plead and beg. And finally she goes."

He pulled away, stared out the window.

"Listen," she said, "I don't expect you to understand."

"Oh, I understand, all right. You're raising her in cotton wool, trying to do the whole thing by yourself. Maybe you *have* to keep her tied to you, but it's not good for either one of you. The kid needs people." He faced her squarely. "So do you."

"You know all about kids, right?" Her voice had risen unexpectedly, sounded angrier than she'd intended. "What makes you an expert?"

"I've had a little experience." He turned on the overhead light and took out his wallet, flipped through the snapshots. "That's Tina—she's a freshman at Yale. Scott's at Pace. I don't say I've done a sensational job, but I know the wrong end of a kid from the part that eats."

"So big deal." She shut off the light, pulled up the emergency brake with a rasping noise. "When I need your advice I'll let you know."

"Touchy tonight, aren't you?" He slammed the door of the car, started down the driveway.

She didn't say good night or look up as she heard his footsteps retreat. They had to work together, they didn't have to be friends. In fact it would be a lot easier to concentrate if they weren't.

She went upstairs and paid Mrs. Binsey, was still seething about Lawton when the woman left. There wasn't any truth in what he'd said. She didn't want to keep Lara all to herself—what kind of craziness was that? The kid needed her.

Lara was awake when Nikki looked in on her, sitting up in bed. She'd sent Lawton home because she wanted to have some time alone with her niece, but now she felt too upset even to talk with her. She bent for a kiss, but Lara pulled away, drawing the quilt to her chin.

"You told me you were working," her niece cried accusingly. "I saw you kissing that man in the car."

Nikki was puzzled till she remembered Lara's habit of looking out the window when she was supposed to be in bed. "You were spying on me!"

"I was waiting for you to come home." Two large tears started on their way down her cheeks and she wiped them away with the back of her hand. "You lied to me!"

"I didn't lie to you—that man was a cop. And you shouldn't be hanging out the window, checking on me. I have my own life to live." And little enough time to live it. "If I catch you doing that again, I'll punish you!"

Nikki backtracked out of the room. Why had she let herself be goaded into a fight? She wasn't making it with anyone tonight. She was upset about the argument with Lawton. But digging deeper, the Sunmann case was driving her crazy. It was as if she didn't have enough brain to go around. This case had been her big opportunity, was going to make her name in the precinct. Instead it was going nowhere.

Once or twice she heard Lara sob. She tried to read the newspaper but couldn't concentrate. Guilt and compassion filled her. She shouldn't have become that angry. If she wanted Lara to feel secure enough to make friends, she shouldn't scream or threaten her.

For no reason at all she suddenly remembered the feel of Lawton's kiss, the roughness and softness of it, her own sense of urgency, her heart beating wildly, out of control. Just thinking about it brought heat to her cheeks.

She rose, forced her thoughts back to Lara, went into the girl's room. Her niece was sound asleep, streaks staining her cheeks where the tears had dried.

She tucked the quilt around her and went to bed herself, feeling like a monster. The kid was going to grow up warped. Nothing she ever did for her seemed right. Yet she loved her—with such an intensity that she wondered sometimes if she could have felt more for a child of her own.

Tomorrow she'd make it up to her, try to explain.

She woke up early the next morning to allow extra time with Lara before school.

"I have a stomachache," her niece said. "Do I have to go?"

"How bad is it?"

"Terrible."

Nikki took her temperature. Normal. Clear eyes and rosy skin. "You have to go."

"But I feel sick—awful." Lara's small hands gripped her belly through the nightgown.

"Come on, honey." She was following the doctor's advice, but she felt like a Gestapo commandant whenever she did. "Get dressed and I'll make you a cup of tea." What if Lara were really sick one day and Nikki forced her to go to school—with a bursting appendix, for instance, or the beginnings of food poisoning? She pushed these thoughts from her mind, gritted her teeth, and went through the routine—tea, a backrub, a hug. "You know I love you, don't you, Lara?"

"Yes, Aunt Nikki."

Last night's anger had been replaced by politeness.

Nikki blamed herself. She'd come down too hard on the kid yesterday.

Nikki ate her corn flakes. "Honey," she said carefully, "I think you misunderstood what you saw last night."

Lara nibbled her toast, her head bent so that none of her face showed.

"When I told you I was working, I was."

Lara put down the unfinished toast. "I'm not hungry."

Nikki was afraid to push the discussion further, worried that Lara's stomach would act up again.

The worst part of any disagreement between them was the loss of trust. Nikki had worked for months to get closer to her. All of that had been lost because of a few minutes' anger. Lara was back inside her shell.

There was nothing she could do about it this morning. She had to get her to school on time, had to go to the station house and start on the Sunmann case again.

She took out her car keys and waited while Lara got her books.

She got to the station house at nine. Eagle-Eye wasn't due in until eleven—it would give her two peaceful hours. Maybe she could get through with her paperwork and escape before he showed. She felt she should have something substantial to show him by now. Yet all she had was a mess of leads that brought her to a dead end. She should have asked him for five days, or at least four. Was today her last day on the case, or was that tomorrow?

The preliminary autopsy report lay on her desk. The bullet holes in Sunmann's body were marked on a diagram. Multiple wounds—three. She already knew that.

The slugs had been sent to the Ballistics lab. One of them was readable—it was from a .38.

She called the License Division, gave them the names of the people involved in the case so far—Sunmann's brother, his friend Arnold, Patty Lumberman, the Bocallis, Denise and Arden Douglas, Ramon Garcia, Rick Kerrigan. Had any of them ever had a .38 registered to them, she asked. The clerk said she'd get back to her within the hour.

The phone rang. It was Mantell, on the desk downstairs. "Young lady here for you, Trakos. Says she knows you. Denise Douglas."

"Send her up."

She heard Denise on the staircase a moment before she came in. Her dark hair fell onto the shoulder of her violet ski jacket. Her face was pale and anxious. Was she angry that Nikki had betrayed her confidences, told Arden about her suspicions? Did she know about it? Or had she come to confess that she really knew Sunmann, had lied?

"I had to talk to you," Denise said. "Arden's planning to go away." Nikki felt her hopes tumble. More evil stepmother stuff. "I heard her say yesterday that as soon as everything settles she's going to travel, that she's never really been anywhere and this would be a good time." Dark rings circled her eyes and her skin had lost its pearly quality.

Denise perched on the edge of a chair, let her shoulder-strap bag fall to the floor. "She's leaving tomorrow," she said. "Don't you think that's awfully fast?"

"How'd you find out?"

"I poked around in her room while she was in the shower."

Nikki gave her a sidelong look. "You really get around."

"I can't let her get away. I found her ticket. She's going to Caracas. I mean, she put on a class act for my father—

that circus at the chapel yesterday—but she couldn't give less of a damn. He isn't even cold." She held her voice in tight control.

"All this has very little to do with who killed Frankie Sunmann," Nikki said.

"Don't you even care what she did to my father?"

"That's not it. I'm on a murder case." At least until my boss takes it away from me.

"Did you ask my stepmother about this man Sunmann?"

"She never heard of him."

"Don't believe her—that's her biggest talent, making up stories."

Nikki picked up a pencil, tapped the eraser end on the desk. "While you're here, I want to clear something up. You told me you hardly spent any time at your father's place—"

"That's right. I'm away at school."

"Your stepmother said you were home over the summer and holidays."

"She's a liar! I can't believe she'd say that!"

Nikki met her glance. "She said some other things, too, about your boyfriend—"

"She hates Rick. She can't wait to tell the whole world how he had a drug problem and was thrown out of school."

"Is it true?"

"What if it is? A lot of the kids play around with drugs. He couldn't handle it, and he messed up."

"Yesterday you said he didn't want you to talk to the cops—why was that?"

The smooth skin between her brows creased. "It's his job—he's . . . on a new job and he doesn't want any problems."

"What kind of problems?"

She looked uncomfortable. "I don't know. Anyhow, he hasn't gone near a drug in months. Why does Arden have to rake all this stuff up now?" Her forehead wrinkled into a dozen fine lines, like silk creasing. "She's trying to draw attention away from herself by pointing at Rick. She's cooking something up—she and that housekeeper."

"Garcia?"

Denise nodded, the dark eyes flashing.

"Did Garcia have a half day off yesterday?"

"I don't know. Rick and I went out after the service. I came in late, and there they were, arguing."

"Arden and Garcia?"

"Yes." She leaned forward. "Arden said, 'If anything leaks out, you won't get a dime.' He looked mad enough to kill. He said, 'It's not enough anyhow.' And then she told him, 'That's all you're getting.' Then they saw me, and Arden asked me what I was doing there—she kind of snapped at me, said I shouldn't sneak up on people. After that it was quiet."

"Garcia claims he doesn't speak English well."

"I know, but that's bull. He understands every word."

Nikki thought of the reports she had to file. If she didn't hurry, Eagle-Eye would be in soon. She pulled back her chair. "Well, thanks for—"

"Aren't you going to do anything at all? Are you just going to let my stepmother walk away?"

"What do you *want* me to do—arrest her? Tell her she can't travel? Look, I'm sorry—"

Denise came to her feet in one swift motion. "I should have listened to Rick. He said the cops don't really give a damn."

"It's way out of my territory. If a crime *was* committed, it belongs to the Coast Guard or maybe the Harbor Police."

"But my father lived in this precinct."

"He died on the water."

"You won't even try to help!" she said bitterly. "Thanks a *lot*."

Nikki saw the pain in her eyes. She had an impulse to say something comforting, to offer advice or help. Before she could, the girl ran into the outer office. She called her name, but Denise didn't look back.

From the doorway Nikki could see her violet jacket slip between the desks and out the door.

15

The girl's anger left a sour taste in her mouth. She couldn't forget her lost, hurt look. Even if Denise had imagined the whole thing, Nikki couldn't help feeling sorry for her; her suspicions were eating her up.

It was still early. Jameson came in carrying a tray of veal and peppers Bernardi's wife had cooked, put it in the half-size refrigerator in the corner.

She tapped an eraser on the frame of Lara's picture, thought about Denise.

The phone rang. "Detective Squad, Trakos."

"Hi." It was Lawton. "Sorry about last night. I shouldn't have told you how to bring up the kid."

"That's okay. It wasn't too cool that I jumped on you, either. Half the time I don't know what I'm doing with her, so it's easy to knock me off balance."

"You're probably doing fine."

"I'm not sure. We had a blowup last night—I've never seen her so mad. And this morning she's being very polite, like we just met."

"She'll be okay."

"Well I'm worried. I can't help it."

"You can't watch them day and night."

She wanted to believe him. It felt strangely comforting

to have someone to talk to about Lara, made her feel calmer.

"What's happening with Sunmann?" he asked.

"I've got some paperwork, and then I thought I'd head into the city, check out Douglas's office. Maybe Sunmann once worked for him, was connected through the job."

Lawton said, "I'm going to get hold of our buddy—the little guy."

"Garcia?"

"Yeah. But first I got some work on this duffel bag case. The wife gave us a name. The creep connects—could be the perp."

"Did you bring him in?"

"A couple of our guys are out there now, looking for him. I'll call you later."

She hung up, tried to concentrate on the reports on her desk. Her mind drifted back to Denise. It was hard to be that young and that angry. Why hadn't she gone to the Coast Guard with her story?

She got up and walked to the window, stared through the glass at the traffic on Coney Island Avenue. Sturgess, one of the clerks, made sure there was water in the plants on the sill. The one in the corner had started to bloom, little red flowers by its shiny leaves.

Suppose there was something to Denise's accusations? Nikki shrugged off the thought—Denise was just a hysterical kid. Yet a minute later Nikki found herself thinking about her old friend Ernie Doblinski, a Coastguardsman.

Ernie was a lieutenant stationed at Floyd Bennett Field. He'd gone fishing on her father's boat every weekend for years. She'd thought he'd retired, but last summer she'd gone to a police seminar down at the field and had bumped into him. He was older and grayer but still working, head of the Records Department.

On impulse, she looked up the number and called.

"Good morning. Brooklyn Operations."

"Lieutenant Doblinski, please." She'd take a minute and satisfy herself. If there was no possibility that Denise's fears were real, she could put them out of her mind and get on with her work.

The deep voice answered, "Doblinski, Records." She could picture his lumpy shape, the piercing blue eyes above the prominent nose.

"Hi, Ernie. It's Nikki Trakos."

"Hey—how's Pop?"

"Good, thanks."

"When you talk to him, tell him I miss him. Ran a damned good boat."

"Thanks, Ernie, I will."

"What can I do for you?"

"I need some information on the Douglas accident for a case I'm working on."

"Hold on, let me get the file." A minute later he was back. "What do you need?"

"How'd the boat explode?"

"They figure he flooded the engine—maybe a gas leak. There wasn't enough of anything left to do a real analysis. The responding crew told him let the motor rest, don't try to start up again right away. I guess he didn't remember."

"But this wasn't his first boat—"

"Listen, even the best guys panic when they can't get the boat to behave. He might've been tired or under stress."

"Ernie, could someone have fooled around with it?"

"You mean deliberately?"

"Right."

"I guess so." He paused. "It'd be pretty hard to

prove at this point. There isn't anything left to investigate."

"How about the insurance people? Don't they send someone down to get the pieces?"

"With a small claim like this, no. It wasn't insured for that much—twenty-five thousand. They have bigger fish to fry."

"How big was the life insurance claim?"

"There wasn't any."

"*What?*"

"I know—it seems crazy. The guy had no insurance on his life. You have to be nuts to live that way today."

Nikki had a prickly sensation at the nape of her neck. Something wasn't right.

"You wouldn't know what company insured the boat, would you?" she asked.

She heard pages turning. "Here it is—Utmost Casualty. Eight thirty-five John Street, in the city."

It was right near where she was going—Barry Douglas's firm was on Water.

She caught herself noting down the information. Why had she done that? If she agreed with Denise that a crime had been committed, why didn't she just tell Doblinski about it, let the Coast Guard handle it? She must be crazy—time was running out on the Sunmann case. Why was she messing around with Douglas?

"They got to him thirty minutes after the call," Doblinski said, "but it was too late. They were busy that night—a commercial yacht lost power, went aground next to the Verrazano." She heard papers rattling on his desk. "Just looking at this Douglas report—helluva way for the guy to go."

"Is there anyone on the rescue crew I could talk to?"

"Jannings handled it, but he's not in right now. Leave

me your number and I'll tell him to call you. Remember, say hello to Pop."

She gave him her number. "Thanks, Ernie."

She'd made the call so she could set aside Denise's hysterical accusations. Instead, she was slowly being sucked into the mystery of Douglas's death. She was intrigued by a man who had lived in a mansion in Manhattan Beach and died without a cent of insurance, a man sharp enough to be called a Wall Street wizard but too dumb to follow the rescue crew's instructions.

Was it possible to make a vessel explode if you were nowhere in the vicinity? She thought of the war movies she'd seen, bridges blown up by remote control devices. If a bridge could be destroyed that way, why not a boat? Or perhaps an explosive with a timer attached had been hidden aboard Douglas's boat before he'd gone out. Had Arden and her lover had help with this one, or had they pulled it off by themselves?

Sunmann's photo stared up at her from a pile of papers on her desk as if to say, Hey, did you forget about me? Was she guilty of the same thing she'd accused Lawton of—paying less attention to Sunmann because he was a "little" case—going for the excitement of the bigger fish?

She pulled the Sunmann papers toward her, shrugged off her guilt, and went back to work.

The laboratory had analyzed the mud on Sunmann's shoes. Neither the mud from the field next to the diner nor the sample from the Bocallis' backyard came anywhere near a match.

She dialed Sam Magliulo, "the Professor," finally reached him, and asked him to come in. Twenty minutes later he was in the office, a short, middle-aged man with an all-year tan and thick hair that looked as though he touched it up with Grecian Formula. His carefully pressed pants were shiny with wear. A bookie and numbers runner, he was connected with organized crime in Brooklyn. The deal was Nikki wouldn't harass him about his illegal activities as long as he kept the information coming.

"Good morning, Detective Trakos." He spoke slowly, used three-syllable words occasionally. He'd once told her he was a college graduate. He sat down and crossed his legs. "Something I can offer you?"

"I'm on a homicide," she said. "Frankie Sunmann."

She could tell by his carefully bland look that he'd heard about the murder, but he said, "Unacquainted with the name." Part of the pretense was to make it seem he knew nothing to begin with, would have to work hard to earn his fee. Nikki tried to keep his prices down because she sometimes paid him from her own pocket.

She showed him Sunmann's picture, but he shook his head. "Not familiar. What do you need?"

"Talk to the two shys he owed and find out what kind of payer he was. Were they having trouble collecting—threatening him, giving him a hard time? Anything like that." The Professor had a small spiral-bound book, too, which he pulled from his pocket. A red one; it made her smile. "The shys' names are Teddy and Fonso," she added.

He looked up. "Those are not pussycats, especially Teddy. I know the gentleman."

"Would he put Sunmann away for not paying?"

"It's a possibility. I'll find out. May take a day or so."

"Soon as you can. Stay in touch."

He gave a brief wave and hurried away.

Jameson went down to the microwave in the basement to heat his veal and peppers. "Want some?" he asked when he got back.

"My God, what time is it?"

"Ten."

"How can you eat so early? Just the smell makes me sick."

"Delicious, mon. Try it."

"Not right now, thanks."

If she wanted to get out of here before Eagle-Eye showed, she'd have to move fast. She placed a call to Pardwick College, spoke to the dean of students. Denise Douglas, it turned out, was an excellent student, a fine musician. She'd given her next of kin as her grandmother, had used that address as her home until six months ago, when her grandmother had died.

"What did she change it to?"

"Just a minute." The dean cleared her throat. "I have a note here that she was going to give us another address, but I see she never did."

Denise might have been telling the truth about avoiding her father's house. In that case she couldn't have been the one Sunmann wanted to see there.

"What about her boyfriend, Rick Kerrigan?" Nikki asked the dean.

"A horse of a totally different color. He had a drug problem, a bad one. Hold on, let me get his record."

He'd seen college as one continual party, had attended classes at whim. Toward the end of his student days he hadn't gone at all. He'd had a running business going in the dorm—pot, cocaine, pills. In fact rumor had it you could order whatever you wanted.

"We had to drop him from the program."

"Did you report him to the cops?"

There was an embarrassed silence. "No. You see, he was going home." Translation: Let the NYPD worry about it. "He promised he'd go into a drug program. Denise swore she'd see to it, and we trusted her. He was only nineteen—we wanted to give him a chance."

A chance to do what, Nikki wondered. Had he straightened out, or was that wishful thinking on Denise's part? She thought of Kerrigan's surly manner and hot temper. If he was still into his drug habit, couldn't he have had some business with Frankie Sunmann three nights ago? She made a note to check him further.

She picked up the paper that held the name and address she'd copied from the motel register: Mr. and Mrs. Amos Johnson, 27500 Moss Lane, Canton, Ohio. "Amos Johnson" was the closest thing to a real suspect she had in the Sunmann case. At any rate he'd been in the Star Garden, had been seen leaving the motel that night. The timing was right to make him the perp. If only she could find him.

She called the Canton police, identified herself, talked to a gravel-voiced detective named Lionburger. "Hold on, please, ma'am. Let me check the phone book real quick for you." A minute later he was back. "Nothing listed, but that doesn't mean much. I'm going to check with the phone company, see if we got an unlisted one for that address, call you right back, ma'am. Talk to you later."

The phone rang ten minutes later. "Detective Trakos? Lionburger here. No unlisted number at that address. I got an inspiration, checked it in the zip code book. Moss Lane is a real street, all right, but the numbers don't go up to twenty-seven five hundred. The highest is eleven five hundred. Someone's playing games with you, ma'am."

"Thanks for your help."

Lawton had been right. "Johnson" had used a phony name.

She rolled a Five into her typewriter—a DD5 Supplementary Complaint Report—the form filled out for every interview carried out by a police officer. She wrote up the results of her phone call to Ohio, typed another for her talk with Denise Douglas. There were more reports to type, three in all. She was a two-finger typist, plugging along till it was done. She dropped everything into Eagle-Eye's Incoming. That should keep him happy.

He was due in any minute. The phone rang as she headed for her jacket and bag. The clerk at the License Division had checked the computer. Two of the names she'd fed into the machine had .38s registered to them: Arden Douglas and Rick Kerrigan. She'd half expected Kerrigan to have a gun. But Arden Douglas? That was a shocker. When was she going to learn there were no surprises on this job?

The phone rang again.

"Stretch?" Lawton sounded tense. "Did you know the little guy was canned?"

"Garcia?"

"Yeah. I called to make sure he'd be at the Douglas place before I ran out there. The widow let him go—"

"What happened?"

"She told me she's trying to save bucks—"

"That doesn't sound right. Denise said she's planning to travel, see the world." She rested her purse on her desk. "Maybe I ought to go out there, get the story straight. There's something else I just found out. She owns a thirty-eight. Registered to her two years ago."

"Hey—"

"It gets even better. Kerrigan, Denise's boyfriend, carries too. His permit's four months old. I'm headed downtown later, to Douglas's office. I thought I'd stop in and ask Kerrigan about the gun—he works a few blocks from there."

"I'll meet you."

"What about the guy they were bringing in on the duffel bag case?"

"They couldn't find him. They're still looking."

She slung her bag over her shoulder. "How do we get hold of Garcia now? Did you get his address?"

"Yeah, from Immigration. He lives in the Bronx, with a daughter. I'm going up there later."

They set a time and place to meet—two o'clock in front of the First Traders, Kerrigan's bank. She gave him the address.

Nikki hung up, thought about Lawton for a second. She opened her bottom drawer, pulled out a pair of spiky black suede shoes, her dressiest. She'd left them in the station house a month ago when she'd come to work straight after a date. A mesh of fine straps, they were a luxury item, not that comfortable to wear—and probably too open for this kind of weather. They'd make her tower over Lawton, but her legs would look curvier. She took a moment to make up her mind, kicked off the practical pumps, slipped on the black suedes, picked up her jacket again.

She'd just started down the stairs when she saw Eagle-Eye on the landing below.

"Trakos!" He came alongside, the light reflecting sharply on his nose. "Glad I caught you. I need a rundown on your homicide."

What could she tell him? That she had a dozen leads that had her running in circles? "Sir, I'm on my way to—"

He took a few steps upward. "Come on up and tell me about it."

He was waiting for her to backtrack and follow him into the office. On what grounds could she refuse? "I would, sir. It's just that my partner—you know, the specialist—arranged his time so I could meet him."

He sniffed as though his air supply had dwindled suddenly. "The homicide guy?"

"Yes, sir. I'm late now." Had he guessed she was lying? He looked grim—or was that the angle? If she'd pushed him too hard, he'd take the case away now, wouldn't wait for her three days to be up.

"Okay, Trakos."

She flew to the bottom of the staircase, was almost through the door when he bellowed, "Trakos, you keeping up with your paperwork?"

"Everything's in your Incoming, sir." She gave him a brief salute, and ran.

16

Arden herself answered the door. Her denim jacket had been run through lots of expensive processes to make it look like a rag. Her red hair was swept into a neat braid that hung jauntily down her back. She held her car keys in her hand.

Nikki explained she had a few more questions.

"Sure," Arden said, "if you don't mind going to Brian's school with me. He missed his school bus—again." She turned back into the house, shouted, "Brian! It won't pay to go soon."

The boy came running from somewhere inside, clutching a stuffed toy in his fist. "I find my coyote," he explained to Nikki, holding up the doll so she could see.

Nikki followed Arden's toast-colored BMW with its vanity license plate—BRIAN—ten blocks to the boy's school, waited while she brought him inside. "I haven't had breakfast," she said when she came out. "Can we do this at a doughnut place near here?"

They walked to the Doughboy Coffee Shop, took a table. After the waitress had set down Arden's order Nikki asked about the gun. "According to our records, Mrs. Douglas, you have a thirty-eight registered to you."

Arden cut the honey-glazed doughnut carefully into quarters, popped one into her mouth, licked her thumb and index finger. "Barry brought the gun home a few years ago.

He thought I should have it. He was working late and I was alone a lot."

"You know how to shoot?"

"He taught me. We'd go out to this firing range and practice."

"When we get back to the house I'll take it so we can—"

"I don't have it anymore. He stopped working late, so he kept it for himself. It was handy when he went night fishing. He didn't like coming into the slip alone in the dark."

"You mean it was on the boat when he had the accident?"

"I'm afraid it was."

Another dead end.

Nikki watched Arden eat her doughnut, wash it down with coffee. She seemed uncomfortable. "I have something to tell you," Arden finally said. "I wasn't exactly honest with you yesterday. About going to the motel to meet this man— you know, when you said Denise had followed me, and I told you I'd never left the house. . . . Well, I did. I was ashamed of it, I guess. I mean, Barry had just died and here I was running out to see some guy. . . ."

Why was Arden volunteering the information now? Nikki wondered. If she'd lied about it to begin with, why not leave it that way?

"I cared for Barry," Arden said, "don't think I didn't. He was good to me. What happened between me and Mitch was something I couldn't stop."

"Mitch?"

"Mitch Robler. He used to work at the racquet club I belong to. We met a couple of years ago, and wham!" She grinned. "I felt like I was sixteen again. I guess I acted that way, too. He was a dream guy—gorgeous. And I went nuts. Barry was working late, all kinds of crazy hours. Mitch taught racquetball. I took lessons with him and then more lessons. Soon it wasn't just racquetball." She laid her napkin on the table, folded it, pressed her nail along the crease. "I would have left Barry then, even though Brian was a baby, but there was a complication—Mitch was married too. His wife was in Canada. He couldn't stand her, but he'd never bothered to end it legally. So we became a thing. And after a while he said he was going up to Canada to get a divorce. He'd come back, I'd leave Barry, and we'd get married."

She swallowed, stirred her coffee. "I didn't hear from him for a whole year—like the earth swallowed him up. Then a month ago, he surfaced. He had the divorce and he was all set. But now *I* was leery. That whole disappearing act bothered me. We couldn't seem to get the relationship back where it was. Part of the trouble was he'd given up his place and was staying with a friend. We couldn't meet there. I kept sneaking out with some excuse and we'd end up in his car like a couple of kids. It started to get sleazy. We were fighting all the time. Finally he decided to rent this motel room so we could have a few days together, figure out what to do. But Brian got sick, and then Barry's accident—"

"Where was Mitch when that happened?"

"At the motel, waiting for me. I had to call and tell him I wasn't coming. He was boiled. And I guess that was the kicker. I went there the next day and blew up, told him he was acting selfish, with no thought for me. He said he'd worked for a year to get free and now it was like he was the last person I was thinking about. We called each other some nasty names. I grabbed my stuff and ran out, figured he'd try to make up, but I didn't hear from him. And the next day when I called the motel, they said he'd gone, left in the middle of the night."

"Where to?"

"I'd give a lot to know. I think he's making me sweat for some of the things I said."

"Did you call the friend he was staying with?"

"I don't have the name or number. He always phoned *me*. I wasn't allowed to call him. That was the way he wanted it."

"What's the name of the racquet club?"

"Gerritsen Health and Racquet Club. But I don't think they'd know where he is. He hasn't worked there in over a year."

Nikki scribbled the name into her memo book. "Mrs. Douglas, who rented the motel room?"

Arden looked surprised. "He did, I suppose. I don't know."

What would Arden say if she knew about the "real sharp-looking piece" who had been with Mitch Robler the day he'd taken the place?

Arden looked at her watch. "I have an errand to do and then I have to be home for Brian's bus."

"My partner tells me you got rid of your housekeeper, Garcia."

"He kept hitting me for more money. I got tired of it." Could that have been the argument Denise had overheard— Garcia asking Arden for a raise? "Anyhow, I'm going away for a few weeks. I won't need him."

"Where are you going?"

"South. For a complete rest. I need to get away."

Funny. If she was as eager to locate Robler as she'd said, why was she leaving?

Arden signaled for a check, took two singles from her wallet.

"One more thing, Mrs. Douglas. You wouldn't happen to have a picture of Mr. Robler, would you?"

Arden flushed under her tan, pulled out a snapshot of a tall blond man in trunks standing at the side of a pool, his arm around a woman in a bathing suit.

"Who's the woman?"

"Marcia Breitson, a friend of mine."

Robler was handsome, photogenic—all muscle. The camera had caught an expression of languid joy on the woman's face as she leaned against him. "I'd like the picture back when you finish with it," Arden said as they walked out. "It's the only one I have."

Nikki made a note of that as she sat alone in her car. She watched the BMW pull away. It would seem that Arden had given her a hot lead. Yet the cop in her was suspicious. Why had she suddenly come forward now? Pangs of conscience because she'd lied? She didn't seem the type.

She glanced at Robler's picture before she tucked it into her purse, noted again the look of ecstasy on Marcia Breitson's face. Robler was a ladies' man, her gut told her. Was he the connection to Sunmann in some way she didn't understand yet?

She stopped at a pay phone, looked up the Gerritsen Health and Racquet Club. A machine answered, but she didn't leave a message. It was twelve-ten. Maybe they were out to lunch. She'd call again later.

She pulled off the Brooklyn Bridge, turned down Park Row. From his pedestal Benjamin Franklin presided stoically over the frantic scene below, people rushing in every direction, street vendors headed for their favorite spots, hoping to catch the lunchtime crowds. She drove through the shadows of John Street all the way to the river, parked at Burling Slip, near the South Street Seaport Museum. Tourists were lined up to visit the *Peking*, the museum's restored square-rigged bark, four masts poking from its deck like giant toothpicks.

She placed her Police Benevolent Association card in plain sight inside the windshield so she wouldn't get a ticket, walked back past the restored brick museum building and shops, turned onto Water Street. The executive offices of Douglas, Roth Associates were in a brand-new skyscraper with a glass and steel facade.

Nikki rode to the twenty-third floor, was buzzed through the plate glass doors, and spoke to the receptionist, a blonde girl who looked too young to be in high school, let alone working. When she found out Nikki was a cop she was flustered.

"Mr. Douglas is— He isn't with us anymore."

"I know that. How about his secretary?"

The girl shook her head. "She's taking a personal day."

Nikki took out Sunmann's picture. "Ever see this man?"

"No, never."

She'd have to come back or call tomorrow. Maybe Douglas's secretary would recognize Sunmann.

She was walking toward the elevator when it occurred to her there might be another answer—Sunmann might have worked for the firm at one time, might have known Douglas then. If so, there'd be a record of his employment.

"Who handles your personnel?" she asked the receptionist.

"That's down on the nineteenth floor."

She waited for the elevator. Four women pushed through the plate glass doors, wearing coats and carrying small cartons, which they plunked down on the carpet. " There isn't much out there," one said, pressing the elevator button. "I looked through the ads on Sunday."

"I'm not going to look till after New Year's," another answered. "Till then I'm living off unemployment."

Had they all been fired? As she rode downward, Nikki remembered Roger Roth telling Arden at the memorial service that he'd "laid off half the staff."

She got out on the nineteenth floor. The carpeting had a flatter pile. The furniture—even the people—seemed more functional.

A middle-aged woman was alone in the first office Nikki came to, packing an open carton on her chair. Inside the carton were small items—framed photographs, a lucite memo holder in the shape of a paper clip, books. The wooden sign on her desk said, "Rhoda Clapper, Assistant Personnel Director," in gilt letters. She glanced at Nikki, turned back to the box, her face narrow under dyed chestnut hair, her mouth tight and angry.

Nikki explained who she was, took out Sunmann's picture. Ms. Clapper looked past her to the doorway. "Maybe someone out there can help you. This is my last day."

"They sent me in here," Nikki lied.

Her mouth flattened into a thin slash. "Wonder what they'll do after I'm gone." She dropped an ashtray into the box, said, "What do you need?"

Nikki showed her Sunmann's picture, spelled his name. "I want to know if he ever worked here."

"Just a minute." Ms. Clapper typed on a keyboard in front of a terminal on her desk, waited. The screen flashed, green letters on a black ground. She shook her head. "Not as far as I can see. Not under that name."

Nikki thanked her, put away the photo. "Seems to be a lot of people leaving."

"Twenty of us. They march you into the boss's office in groups of five, give it to all of you at once. Like a firing squad." Her mouth twisted. "I wouldn't mind if it was fair, but it's not. Four years I've been with this lousy firm. You'd think they'd keep me, let some of the newer people go. But no, I was in the first group."

"I'm sorry. Company losing money?"

Ms. Clapper smirked. "I guess you haven't heard. It's all because of that great genius, Barry Douglas. I don't like to speak ill of the dead, but God forgive me, the man was a crook. He lifted ten million bucks from the discretionary accounts—disappeared it."

Usually it was hard to break down an employee's loyalty, get information about company affairs. But anger was a great help in getting people to talk. Nikki asked, "Didn't Roth know about the ten million?"

"He knew last month, but Douglas said he just borrowed it to buy some hot issue and was going to put it all back. Between you and me, if Douglas hadn't killed himself, Roth would've killed him. His cute little tricks are pulling the firm under."

"What are discretionary accounts?"

"That's when a customer turns money over to a broker and gives him permission to trade without consulting the customer. You have to be crazy, but a lot of people do it."

"They must've trusted Douglas—"

"He made a lot of money for his people. So no one ever questioned him. Last month when the statements went out showing the withdrawals he told the customers it was a computer error and that it would get cleared up next month. But Roth knew."

"Didn't he care?"

"He was used to it. Douglas was always swinging capital around, investing in stuff. Roth figured Douglas would stand by his word. Douglas told him to think of the money as a short-term loan, that he'd put it all back." She snorted. "Some loan!"

"What happened to the money?"

She shrugged her shoulders, long hoop earrings swinging forward. "Gone with the wind. Roth talked to Mrs. Douglas about it, but she says she knows nothing."

Ten million. Even half that amount would have given Arden and her boyfriend a juicy motive to kill. Assuming that Arden knew how to get her hands on the money.

Ms. Clapper stood and pitched another book into the carton. "That's life," she said bitterly. "Some of us are born smart and the rest have to scrounge."

Nikki waited for the elevator, her internal alarm buzzing loudly. Douglas had embezzled ten million—enough to keep him in gravy for the rest of his life. And where was he? At the bottom of the sea? Her gut told her no. His body hadn't been found. What proof was there that he'd died? What if he'd engineered his own "death" in a fake accident, planned it so he could disappear and start life somewhere else under a new identity? With a ten-million-dollar nest egg.

She found a phone and dialed the precinct. Jameson told her she'd had a call from the Coast Guard—Ensign Jannings had left his number. The Coastguardsman who'd handled the Douglas rescue operation. Just the man she wanted to talk to.

Jannings sounded young, with a trace of Southern softness in his voice. She explained who she was, then asked, "What can you tell me about the Douglas accident?"

"A bad scene. We got to him about seven o'clock. We saw the man—had him in our lights, and then it was all over in a second."

"You say you *saw* him?"

"That's right, ma'am. We were about two hundred yards away. He was bending over the controls, trying to get them to work, I guess. He was wearing something dark, and he had one of those hats on his head with the gold trim—"

"A yacht cap?"

"Yes. We were hoping he'd have his life preserver on, but he didn't. We tell them that first thing when we get a call: 'Put on your life jacket and wait for us.' But I guess he didn't expect the whole thing to go like that, right away. It went up like the Fourth of July, just when we were coming in on him."

"You looked for him?"

"Sure did. We figured maybe he was blown clear or grabbed something and stayed afloat—there was a mess of wood and fiberglass in the water. But all we came up with was the hat. We looked for hours—another boat helped us till the backup crews showed."

"A Coast Guard boat?"

"No, private."

"Which one?"

"The *Flora*, that was her name. They saw the fire, came in to see what they could do."

She thanked Jannings and hung up, scribbled the name "*Flora*" in her memo book. There went another theory. Jannings had seen Douglas go down with the boat. If anyone were to benefit from the embezzled ten million it would probably be Arden and her lover, not Douglas himself.

She didn't want to think about Arden, didn't want to focus on the Douglases at all. She should be concentrating on Sunmann; why did she keep getting dragged in other directions?

She glanced at her watch. She had a half hour before she met Lawton, too little time to do anything on the Sunmann case anyhow. Douglas's insurance broker was only a few blocks away, on John Street. She'd stop in and have a little talk. You never knew what you'd learn.

Ben Teitelman of Utmost Casualty was an aggressive, old-style insurance salesman, close to retirement age or even beyond it.

She showed him the picture of Sunmann on the off chance that there might be a connection, but Teitelman had never seen or heard of Sunmann. He was more than willing to talk about Barry Douglas. His frustration at failing to sell Douglas life insurance was driving him crazy.

"He never let me bring it up. The idea of dying depressed him." He talked with his hands, a gold filigree ring picking up the light as he gestured. He had a full head of white hair and a ruddy complexion.

"I got lots of customers like Barry. Don't want to think about dying. That's why it's hard to sell life insurance." Teitelman's desk was stacked with colored binders. He had the corner space and the largest window in a room divided into cubicles; Nikki guessed he had seniority.

The Brooklyn Bridge was framed in the window. Afternoon sunlight touched its gray towers, sparkled on the cables. "I feel terrible. Look at the mess the family's in now—a man goes and they're left on their own."

"You carried the rest of his insurance?"

"That's right. The house, the car, the boat."

"Did he have any trouble getting boat insurance?"

"If you mean did he have a past record of accidents, the answer is no. You could have knocked me over when this happened. He'd been running a boat for years, ever since I can remember. This one he bought two years ago, new. Had it fitted out with all the latest gadgets. That was Barry—only the best."

"You know him a long time?"

His cheek lifted in a half smile. "A thousand years, my dear. I insured his *father* when Barry was just a little cocker. His folks had a hardware store on Flatbush Avenue. Yeah," he said sadly, "they passed away a long time ago." He tipped back abruptly in his swivel chair. "And now Barry's gone, too. So young—forty-two. Want some coffee?"

"No, thanks."

Teitelman swiveled to the automatic coffee maker behind him, pulled a Styrofoam cup from a stack on a tray.

"He came a long way from Flatbush Avenue," Nikki said.

"He was a sharp kid, the kind who was figuring out how to make big bucks in the market while his friends were still playing stickball. I remember once he worked at Macy's for Christmas. He told his father he could figure fifteen different ways to rip off the store. 'Don't worry,' he said, 'I'm not going to do it, but their system stinks. It's full of holes.' "

No wonder he'd turned to crime. He'd shown early talent.

"His father worried about him. Too smart, he used to say. 'Ben,' he'd tell me, 'someday that kid'll ruin himself.' But he didn't have to worry. Barry turned out all right. More than all right. Made a pile of dough."

And if he'd practiced a little larceny as he plied his trade, that didn't matter, did it?

He poured coffee, dropped a cube of sugar into it. "Smart, smart, smart," he said, "and in the end, stupid. Why didn't he insure his life? I mean, here you have a family—a beautiful wife and baby—and you leave them uncovered? And there's another kid, a girl from his first marriage. I wanted to say, 'Come on, Barry, grow up.' But you couldn't talk to him. And he was nuts about his wife."

Nikki felt her attention sharpen. "They'd been married a long time?"

"No. About five, six years. He went in for a hernia operation; she was his nurse. It turned him upside down. He was married then, and he broke it up and went after her. That's the way he was. He saw something, he had to have it."

"He didn't have her long."

"No. A shame, just a terrible shame. And look how he left her. He used to turn me off when I'd start talking about coverage. 'Ben,' he'd say, 'don't worry. I'll provide for them in my own way.' Well, if he did, I don't know about it. Maybe he was going to, and then this happened. Left them without a nickel."

Lawton was impressed with the size of Barry Douglas's theft. They waited in the inner offices of First Traders Bank, where Rick Kerrigan worked. They'd asked for Kerrigan but he was on an errand. James Madden, a bank vice-president who was Kerrigan's boss, was in a meeting but would see them soon. "Ten million bucks isn't bad," Lawton said.

"Arden says she doesn't know where the money is." She leaned back in an armchair, crossed her legs. The shoes *did* look nice, the thin straps showing off her ankles.

"What'd you expect her to say? Douglas probably had a numbered Swiss account or a bunch of bonds tucked away somewhere. Maybe she and this guy Robler whacked him so they could live happily ever after—on the bread he stole. She could be headed there now, to get the money."

He stood, stretched, paced restlessly, hands in the pockets of his navy blazer. His jaw was starting to darken; his morning shave lasted only till afternoon. He perched on the arm of the sofa near her. "This stuff you found out about Douglas's widow—what the daughter told you, what you found out at his company—you should give it over."

"To the Coast Guard?"

"Yeah, or the Harbor Police. Call and find out who's working on it."

"I guess I should."

She felt resistance to the idea, though she wasn't sure why. Maybe she wanted to be the one to help Denise Douglas. Or maybe she wanted to solve both cases at once, be a hotshot. As a kid she'd had this vision of herself as Superwoman, ridding the city of corruption, avenging every crime, the cape flowing behind her. Maybe it was time to take off the costume.

"I'll check into it tomorrow," she said, "pass it along."

Madden came out of his office, a tall, loose-jointed man in his late forties, wearing narrow half-glasses over dour features. His meeting was still going on, but he'd taken a break so he could talk to them. He'd hired Rick Kerrigan six months ago to carry valuables between the bank's branches. He sent for Kerrigan's job application, showed it to them. Nikki was interested to see that it made no reference to Pardwick College. The last entry under "Education" was St. Joseph's, a parochial high school in Bensonhurst. Kerrigan had simply omitted his whole college experience. No wonder he'd been edgy when Nikki had asked where he worked.

"Rick in some kind of trouble?" Madden asked.

"Just checking him out," she said.

"What's it all about?"

She explained about the Sunmann case, how Kerrigan tied in.

Madden's expression darkened. "To tell you the truth, the kid's got a hot temper. He was involved in a brawl a couple of months ago. I had to cool him down."

"What was the fight about?"

Madden looked at them over his half-glasses. "The bank's very tight on its drug policy, fires anyone caught using stuff. We found a bag of coke in the locker room and the janitor said it was Rick's. Rick started swinging at the guy and it took two of us to pull him off."

"*Was* it his?"

"We couldn't prove it."

"Any more drugs since then?"

"No."

"How's his work?"

"That's the thing—it's fine. Always on time, stays late if he has to, takes the job seriously. A little rough around the edges but trying hard."

Nikki asked about the gun. Carrying it had been one of the requirements for the job. Kerrigan needed it when he delivered cash and bonds. He'd applied for a permit four months ago, had gotten it with no trouble.

Madden had just finished talking when the outer door opened and Kerrigan came in, wearing a gray blue uniform that looked too tight for his muscled torso. His eyes narrowed when he saw them. His jaw became rocklike and his high color shaded to a dull rust. "What is this?" He looked at Nikki. "What're you doing here?"

"It's about your gun."

"What about it?"

"We're going to need it for a few days."

"What! Hey—what the hell's going on?"

"Sunmann was put away with a thirty-eight, same caliber as yours."

Beads of sweat broke out on his forehead. "I told you I don't know shit about the Sunmann guy."

The ridges in Madden's forehead deepened. "Cool it, Rick. All you have to do is be straight with them."

"Mr. Madden, I swear I don't know what the hell this is all about."

"Let them have the gun." His voice was tense, as if he were talking to an unruly child. "We can switch your schedule till you get it back."

Kerrigan looked uncertain.

"Go on, Rick."

He pulled the gun from its shoulder holster and dropped it into Nikki's hand. A .38. Small but powerful.

"So that's that." Madden's lips compressed. "Come in later, and we'll go over your schedule." He nodded to Lawton and Nikki, returned to his office.

Kerrigan's face was livid. He glared at the wall as though he wanted to put his fist through it. "You had to come here, didn't you?" His fists clenched and the powerful muscles under his jacket bunched. "Had to show me up in front of my boss, make him wonder about me. I got enough trouble here—people picking on me, making up stories."

Nikki said, "Why'd you leave Pardwick off your application?"

"He showed you that? He had no right—"

"You wrote it as though you never went to college—"

"What do you think, lady, I should've told him all about me—that I was a needlehead, a druggie?" His voice became a frantic whisper. "It's none of his fucking business. But I suppose *you* filled him in," he said bitterly. "People are always ready to screw you. The sick thing is I haven't gone near a drug in eight months. I'm finally doing the right thing. And now this."

Lawton said, "Hey, you're making a mountain out of it."

"If I lose my job, it'll be your fault, mister. You and your girlfriend's."

Nikki asked, "Where were you Monday night—about eleven, twelve o'clock?"

"You're not going to hang this shit on me! I was with Denise, that's where. I've been with her *every* night since her father died. If you don't believe me, ask her."

Denise would back Kerrigan to her grave.

Kerrigan gripped the doorknob. "Get yourself another fall guy, lady." The glass rattled in the door as he slammed it.

Nikki scooped up her jacket and purse. "You believe he's clean?"

Lawton was still looking at the door. "I don't know. He's working awful hard to convince us."

They sped up the FDR Drive, passed a tug pushing a barge up the East River, exited at Twenty-third Street. The ballistics lab was housed in the Police Academy building on East Twentieth, an unassuming gray structure that looked like an urban high school, discreetly closed off from the street by a bordering hedge.

They pushed past blue-jacketed cadets, went upstairs. They waited while the gun was test-fired and the slug compared to one taken from Sunmann's body. Only one of the slugs was readable—the other two were badly deformed. The test bullet was "miked," placed under the microscope, and compared with the murder bullet. If they carried the same markings, that would prove they'd come from the same barrel. The search would be narrowed significantly. They'd have a murder weapon and a probable killer, could direct their energies to finding a motive.

While they waited for test results, Nikki found a phone, called the Gerritsen Health and Racquet Club again. A rough-voiced man answered. When she asked for information on Mitch Robler the man said impatiently, "Who is this?"

"Detective Trakos of the—"

"Hey, I *thought* someone would put a detective on that bum sooner or later. He deserves it. Some husband probably hired you to find Mr. Hotpants, wants to take him out of the picture, right?" He'd mistaken her for a private detective. She didn't correct him.

"Do you have an address for Robler?"

"I don't. If I had I would've gone there myself and

ripped him limb from limb. He took off a year ago with five hundred dollars' expense money he was supposed to spend on athletic equipment. Left without a good-bye. I can tell you the last place he lived. Hold on a minute." Nikki heard papers rattling. "Ten-fifty Bergen Beach Avenue. But if anybody might know where he is, that's Marcia Breitson. Is it her husband who hired you?"

"I'm not free to say. Could you give me Mrs. Breitson's number—might be a lead."

"Sure. It's 882-7360. If you get the husband, watch out. When he hears Robler's name he turns into an animal. Good luck—if you find the bastard, let me know."

No one answered at the Breitson residence.

Nikki and Lawton went back upstairs to Ballistics and were waiting when the technician came out and handed back the gun. "Sorry, wrong number," he said. "No match in any way."

She looked at Lawton. "Would've been too easy, I guess."

"I tell you," Lawton said as they got into the elevator, "I never had the big guy figured for this one. I like the little guy better."

"Garcia?"

"Yeah. Let's head up to the Bronx, and see what he knows."

He called his office before he left. "No luck on the duffel bag case yet," he told her. "They can't find the guy. They're going to leave it alone till tomorrow—they have a lead on where he'll be in the morning."

17

They got back onto the FDR. Manhattan's towers rose to the left of the drive, clustered spikes reflecting twilight, the Citicorp's roof, a giant slide, poked the sky. Joggers ran near the river, breath steaming in the suddenly chill air. Under the Queensborough a tramway car was heading toward Roosevelt Island.

They turned onto the Willis Avenue Bridge. Ahead lay the Bronx, gray and mysterious, where Garcia and his daughter lived.

Lawton tooled the Fury with one hand. "So where are we on Sunmann? Looks like a stinker—no solid leads, no handle yet."

"What about his mood? He was onto something the night before he died." She adjusted her window. "His landlord told me he came running down the steps like he was going into orbit."

"So what do you think got him souped up?"

"His friend Greenberg might know."

"The fat guy?"

She nodded. "Could be Sunmann mentioned something Greenberg doesn't remember. I'm going to ask him to do a replay—exactly what they did Sunday night. Maybe something'll come back to him."

They pulled off the Cross Bronx Expressway. Lawton

stopped for a light near a group of leather-jacketed teen-agers on a corner, clicked down the car locks.

They passed blocks and blocks of abandoned buildings that looked bomb struck. Steel sheets painted with deco-rative scenes covered missing windows, hid the emptiness inside—pictures of curtains, flowers, cats, shutters. She knew what really lay behind the fake windows—rats and filth, breeding places for crime.

Thirty-four Seventy Clinton Avenue, where Garcia lived, was ancient and graffitied, but at least it was occupied. Some windows were cracked. Towels and rags had been stuffed into the sashes to keep out the draft.

An old man sat on the stoop, his face carved out of yellowed mahogany, bluish around the lips. It was cold, but all he wore was a badly frayed tweed sport jacket with one button missing. Above his head a bulb burned in a wire cage against the old brick.

Nikki had the feeling as they passed that he knew they were cops. If not cops, some kind of authority figures, maybe social workers or health department inspectors. This building had seen its share of them, she was sure. She followed Lawton across the paper-strewn courtyard, through the heavy steel-barred door with half its plate glass missing.

The smell of the lobby hit her right away—stale grease and urine. In spite of the breeze from outside, the odor was thick and pungent, as though it had been laid in with the chipped mosaics of the floor.

The light above the mailboxes wasn't working. Lawton flicked on a match, moved it along the name slots. The boxes were bent and damaged, with few names to mark whose they were. None of them said Garcia. "Welcome to the Taj Mahal," he commented.

"There's no building directory. I wonder where the

super lives." A noise made her turn. The old man was watching them from the dimness a few feet away.

"Know where Garcia lives?" Lawton asked.

He shrugged narrow shoulders. "*No sé.*"

"I bet he'd *sé* if he saw a little green," she said, opening her purse.

Lawton reached into his pocket before she could pull out her money and offered a folded ten. "Ramon Garcia," Lawton said.

"Two C." The man stuffed the bill into his jacket, pointed to the staircase on their right.

The walls along the dirty marble steps were graffitied— "Tony and Geri" inside the outline of a heart, "Marie sucks," "Bandidos."

"You overpaid," she whispered as they walked up. "Could have bought it for five."

"Think of it as an investment. We may need him."

The door of 2C had an empty name slot. Lawton rang the bell and waited, but no one answered. Finally he knocked, hard. Nikki heard a tapping noise as someone came forward, saw a flicker behind the peephole. A young woman said, "Yes, who is it?" Tense and wary, but no trace of accent.

"Police."

"Just a minute."

A pause. Footsteps retreated inside the apartment. A TV suddenly became louder. More footsteps. Lawton looked at Nikki, then shouted at the peephole, "What the hell's going on? Open the door!" A door opened to their right. Two dark-eyed children stared out from behind it. Down the hall another door opened. A dog barked noisily.

Lawton rattled the knob and banged on the metal with the flat of his palm. "What the hell?"

Nikki was about to suggest that one of them cover the

back of the building when the door opened. A chain held it to a gap of less than a foot. At first glance the woman behind it seemed like a girl because everything about her was so delicate. She was in her early twenties, slim and small-featured, shining black hair cut so that it swung forward in twin wings toward her chin. "Show your ID," she said.

"ID my ass!" Lawton yelled. "Let us in."

The woman pretended to be fumbling with the chain. After what seemed like minutes she finally unlatched it. Lawton pushed past, almost knocking her over.

"Wait a minute, mister!"

He ran into the apartment, his footsteps echoing on the linoleum.

The woman cried in a high, piping voice, "Son of a bitch! You can't just run all over the place!"

"You don't like it, call a cop!"

He poked his head into two front rooms, ran down the long hallway to the back. Nikki followed into a neat bedroom. A cool breeze blew in from the window. Lawton rushed across, pushed aside the billowing curtain. "That's how the bird flew," he said. "Heard us and ran."

The sash was raised high. Nikki leaned out, looked up and down. A fire escape led to an empty alley strewn with litter and broken pavement. No one was in sight.

"Enjoying the scenery?" the woman snapped from behind them.

They pulled back, stood facing her across the neatly made beds. A bronze crucifix hung high on the wall. Lawton's breath was coming fast, his cheeks flushed. "You let him get away."

"Who?" Her slanting black eyes glittered with hostility.

"Come on, let's not play. You Garcia's daughter?"

"That's right." She looked like Garcia except that on

her the sleek darkness was attractive. She wore a simple blouse and pants that showed off her tiny waist, flat stomach. "What's this about?"

"Your name?"

"Felicia."

"Okay, Felicia, let's cut the crap and talk about your father."

"He's not here."

"I can see that. You going to answer some questions or do we put you down as uncooperative?"

She hesitated, her eyes calculating. She didn't look like an amateur at this. She'd talked to plenty of cops before, Nikki guessed. Her face became resigned. She seemed annoyed at the imposition, not in the least worried. She turned without a word and clicked back down the linoleum. They followed her into a living room near the entry. The TV blasted, unwatched. She turned off the set and sat down. She picked up an emery board, filed her thumbnail.

The room was immaculate. The Oriental rug, though worn in patches, was dustless. The mahogany furniture was old but cared for. A scratch mark on the arm of the sofa where Lawton and Nikki sat had been filled and the wood glowed with polish. A photo stood on the lace doily covering the sideboard—Ramon and Felicia with an older woman and three younger children in a family group.

One of the sofa cushions showed an indent, as if recently used. A thin brown cigarillo burned in an ashtray on the coffee table.

"Where's your father?" Nikki asked.

"I don't know. I haven't seen him in weeks."

Nikki's glance moved meaningfully to the cigarillo, and Felicia snatched it up, held it awkwardly in her fingers for a few seconds, then moved the ashtray to an end table near her and put it in that. "Why do you want him?" she asked, emery board poised in midair. Not a trace of Hispanic inflection. Her voice was steady and she met Nikki's glance evenly.

"What does your father know about a man named Frankie Sunmann?"

"Who?" Her forehead wrinkled and she seemed puzzled.

Nikki took out Sunmann's picture, laid it on the coffee table.

"Never saw him before. What's he got to do with us?"

"That's what we want to know. He had your father's address in his pocket when he died the other night. He was murdered."

Her eyes shot open. The emery board slipped from her fingers, fell between the cushions of the couch. Whatever Garcia knew about Sunmann's death, he hadn't mentioned it to her. "Wait a minute—he had this address on him?"

"No, your father's work address, in Brooklyn."

"The Douglas place?"

"Yes."

Her frown deepened. Her finger went to a cross on a slender chain around her neck, slid it back and forth.

"Where's your father, Ms. Garcia? Why'd he run when we came?"

"He didn't run! He was never here!"

Nikki eyed the cigarillo again. Felicia caught her glance and snatched it up awkwardly. She put it to her lips and took a small puff, careful not to inhale. Her fingers were pale and clear, unstained by nicotine, the nails lacquered. "My father's a hard-working man, decent man. He never did a bad thing in his life. All he wants is to save enough to bring my mother and the kids up from Ecuador. That's why we live in this dump, why he's doing housework—

he's not ashamed." It sounded like a set speech, one she'd given often.

"How long has he been in the States?"

"Three years. Mr. Douglas brought him up here."

"How'd he get the job?"

"*I* got it for him, if you want to know. I thought it would be a chance for him to make good money. Mr. Douglas owns—owned the company where I work."

"You work for Douglas, Roth?" Nikki asked.

"That's right. Hey, how'd you know the name?"

"What do you do there?"

She bent so that the wings of her hair covered her face, crushed out the cigarillo. "I'm a secretary. A few years ago Mr. Douglas asked me if I knew someone who could train as a houseman. My father spoke a little English, and he was willing to do anything to get a start. It sounded like a good deal. Mr. Douglas brought him up from Ecuador, paid his air fare, all his expenses. It was right after Mr. Douglas's kid was born."

She recrossed her legs. A gold ankle chain gleamed under the nylon. "I lived with my aunt before that. My father came up and we got this place. It seemed to be working out okay. But now I find out that Mr. Douglas was a crook—he stole millions of dollars from the company. I never meant to get my father mixed up with a man like that."

Lawton got up, paced restlessly to the doorway. Nikki caught his glance, signaled him with a tiny nod that he could carry the ball if he wanted to. "Lady," he said, "let's stop the crap. What was your father's work address doing in this guy Sunmann's pocket?"

"I don't know." Her eyes were dark as coal, impenetrable. "Anyhow, he doesn't work there anymore. He quit." Nikki could have sworn Lawton had said Garcia'd been fired.

"When?"

"Yesterday."

"I thought you didn't see him."

"He called this morning."

"From where?"

She shrugged, small breasts lifting under her blouse. "He didn't say. He's a grown man—I don't keep tabs on him."

"Why'd he quit? He have a fight with the widow?"

"No. Nothing like that."

"Then what?"

She concentrated on an invisible piece of lint on her pants.

"Maybe you got it wrong," Lawton said. "Maybe she threw *him* out."

She shrugged, as though it mattered too little to think about it.

"Maybe she caught him with the silverware and got rid of him."

"My father would never steal! That's why he left. He doesn't want to work for people like that."

"People like what?"

She hesitated for a beat. "I told you. Mr. Douglas stole from the company."

"And Mrs. Douglas?"

She lifted a shoulder. "My father didn't explain. He just said he was leaving."

"He have anything else lined up?"

"He's going to be busy going down to get my mother and the kids."

"He has enough?"

"He will have."

Had Garcia come into money suddenly? How? Nikki thought back to what Denise had overheard—Arden telling Garcia, "If anything leaks out, you won't get a dime," and Garcia answering, "It's not enough."

"Where's he going to get the money from?" Lawton asked.

Her shoulder lifted again.

"Did he tell you what he was into?"

"He's into nothing! He wouldn't do anything wrong. He's an honest man, a good man."

"Then where's he getting the money from?"

She wet her lips with a flick of her tongue. "Mrs. Douglas owes him. She promised him a bonus he never got."

"How much?"

"He didn't say." She rose abruptly. "That's all I know." She walked into the hallway, unlatched the door.

Nikki gave a tiny nod to tell Lawton she was ready to leave. They walked to the door.

Lawton pulled a card from his pocket. "If you hear from your father, call me."

"You're wasting your time, mister."

"Let *me* decide."

The chain rattled against the jamb as the door slammed.

"Tough cookie," Lawton remarked.

They walked down the steps. "I wonder where Garcia went," Nikki said.

"Back to the widow to get what she owes him. Except it's not a bonus."

"Maybe he found out Arden's boyfriend did Sunmann and he's blackmailing her. Or else he did Sunmann himself and wants to get paid."

"Okay—all we need now is why."

The old man was still there when they came out. A boy a little older than Lara—ten or eleven—was with him. Lawton asked the man, "Did Garcia come out of here?"

The boy interpreted and the man nodded vigorously. "*Sí.*" A barrage of Spanish followed.

"He come from the alley," the boy translated. "He run that way. 'Bout ten minutes ago."

He was pointing to the subway el several blocks away. They'd never catch him.

Lawton asked the old man, "What kind of guy is this Garcia—good, bad? Trouble with the cops?"

The boy translated again. The old man listened intently and then spoke, his eyes hard. Nikki caught the word *policia*.

"He say he work hard, this Garcia, save every penny." The boy grinned. "He say he squeeze the nickels. He got a wife and kids in Ecuador. He and the daughter, you know, they save to bring the family here. But he say he do *anything* for money. Bring trouble to the building. Couple years ago he sell stolen guns. No one can prove, but everyone know he do it. The daughter, she lie for him. Then one day a kid in the building, he do a holdup with a gun he buy off this Garcia, and he get in trouble. The store guy is shot. All the people get together and tell Garcia he gotta stop or move. So now, you know, he's clean. But that don't mean nothing. He and the daughter, they keep to themselves." And then, as an afterthought, "No one mess with him. He know how to take care of himself."

"He has a gun?" Lawton asked.

The boy turned to the old man, repeated the question in Spanish. "He don't know for sure," the boy said. "He think maybe."

They were starting toward the Fury when the old man added something else.

"He say *he* save money for *his* family, too," the boy said.

Nikki was undecided for a moment. Lara needed new clothes—she seemed to grow an inch every time Nikki looked away from her. She tried hard to watch her budget. But the old man's hands were raw from the cold, his thin collar pulled up against the wind.

She reached into her bag and handed him a ten.

When they were out of earshot Lawton said, "You could have let me handle it."

"It was my turn."

"I thought you said I gave him too much to begin with."

"What the hell, I'm not even sure why I did it."

He opened the car door for her, slipped inside and warmed the motor.

She glanced at him across the divider, saw his slanted grin.

18

It was raining by the time they reached Brooklyn. Lawton parked a block from the Douglas house. The branches of the willows thrashed in the wind, their boughs bent to the lawn. The path between the trees gleamed eerily.

"What makes you so sure Garcia'll come back here?" she asked.

"Where else would he go? The widow owes him money, maybe a big bundle."

"We might have missed him. We left his house later than he did."

"Trust me." Lawton turned off the motor but left the key in it. "It has to take longer by subway than by car."

They'd raced back, but even so, they'd hit early rush-hour traffic. It was five, past the time she usually phoned Lara, but she hadn't had time to stop before, and there was no way she could get out and make a call now. "I feel bad that I didn't call my niece."

"You worried about her?"

"No—not that she won't be taken care of. But she was so down this morning. I hate to see her that way."

"She's probably out with her friends, forgot all about it."

"This kid has no friends. Just me."

He seemed about to say something, hesitated.

"Go ahead," she said. "I won't bite your head off."

"I was going to say lighten up, don't focus on her. You're worried. She sees that. Now she's worried, too."

It was too simple an explanation for all of Lara's troubles. But maybe there was some truth in it. "It's worth a shot." Anything was.

They waited half an hour longer. Nikki wondered if the time could have been better spent. Rain pelted the windshield, cut visibility. Twin lights burned on either side of the doorway, but the house itself was dark, at least the windows that fronted the street. What if no one was home? What if Lawton was wrong?

Suddenly he came alert. "Oops. Here we go."

She looked around. She'd missed Garcia. He scurried from the direction of the bus stop, head down, hands dug into pockets. He ran up the path and lifted the brass knocker. A minute later the door opened. Arden was silhouetted against the entry. She didn't seem happy to see him, tried to shut the door, but he pushed his way inside.

After ten minutes Lawton checked his watch. "First she tries to shut the door in his face and now they're going to make a night of it."

"No—here he comes."

Garcia emerged, pulled up his jacket collar, and ran down the path.

Lawton let him turn the corner before he started the car. He followed skillfully, careful not to alert him. At Emmons, Garcia boarded a bus. Lawton pulled up close. "Shit! I hope we don't lose him."

They tailed the bus, inspecting the passengers who got off at each stop. At Coyle Street, Garcia jumped down and turned north. Lawton gave him plenty of room.

"He's headed back toward where Sunmann was killed," Nikki pointed out.

Minutes later he ran into the office of the Star Garden Motel.

"I'll be damned," Lawton said. "What's he doing there?"

He came out a minute later, moving quickly beneath the overhang along the bottom row of rooms.

Lawton parked across the street. "He may be going to see someone."

"Who? No one else is parked in the lot, and there aren't any lights on."

"Maybe he rented a room," he said.

Wouldn't Bender have turned him away? She thought of how Garcia looked—alone, rain soaked, with no car or luggage. Then she remembered how empty the motel was, how desperate Bender had seemed for clients. Bender would rent to E. T. if he had money.

Garcia stopped at 19, the last room on the lower floor, off by itself, and inserted a key in the lock. As soon as he'd slipped inside and shut the door she and Lawton eased out of the car and walked along the paved strip. She remembered how Lawton and Garcia seemed to light sparks in one another at the memorial service. "If it's okay," she said, "I'll take this one."

"You're sure?"

She nodded.

"He's all yours."

Nineteen was separated from the others by the laundry area, empty now except for two rusting washing machines and a dryer. She felt keyed up, edgy.

Both she and Lawton drew their guns. Following standard procedure, they separated, standing on either side of the door. Last week in East Harlem a cop had been gunned down through a locked door, a reminder that procedures were followed for good reason.

She knocked.

"Who is it?" Garcia growled.

"Room service. Clean towels."

He hesitated so long she wasn't sure he was going to

open. Then the door moved fractionally. When he saw them, he tried to push it shut, but Nikki was too fast. She threw her weight against it. It slammed his elbow and he stumbled backward.

"*Mierda!*"

The loathing in his face deepened when he saw Lawton. He turned to Nikki, rubbing his elbow. "What you want?"

"To talk to you."

Terror flew across his face, hid behind a sullen mask. "I don't know nothing." Lines of exhaustion showed in the deep creases between his nose and mouth. His complexion was a slick yellow brown, like dirty clay.

She put her gun back into its holster but left her jacket open so it would be within easy reach. They moved into the room. Lawton shut the door. The bed was covered with a flowered spread that didn't match the stripe in the curtain or the swirls in the cheap carpeting. A small pinup lamp spread a yellow, murky light.

"How you find me?" Garcia asked.

"Followed you, from your daughter's house."

His face narrowed like a reptile's. "*Culea de mierda!* Fucking shit! Felicia know nothing!"

He glared at them, water still running from the strands of his hair onto his wet shirt and soggy pants. His lips thinned and he turned away, dried himself with a towel. The panic in his eyes was just below the surface.

He hung his soaking jacket on the doorknob, toweled his hair and face. Beads of sweat lined his upper lip.

Nikki sat near Lawton on a plastic-covered armchair next to the bed and waited while Garcia lit a cigarillo.

She took out her memo book. "Why'd you run when you heard us, up in the Bronx?"

He ran his tongue over his teeth, said nothing.

"Why'd you climb through the window and take off?"

It was like questioning a brick wall. Lawton clenched his fists as though he wanted to belt him.

"Hey, macho man," she said to Garcia, "maybe you'd be more comfortable down at the precinct."

The look in his eyes was naked rage, humiliation at being spoken down to by a woman. But he held himself in check. She was a cop—if he allowed instinct to take over, she could make infinite trouble for him. "I talk here."

She felt chilled by the fury she'd glimpsed, glad to have her gun and Lawton as backup. "I asked why you ran away," she said evenly.

"In my country, police no good people."

That was probably as good as she was going to get. She looked around. Why had he rented a room? He'd just taken a two-hour subway and bus trip in the rain—he wasn't the kind to spend on his own comfort. The old man had said he "squeezed the nickels."

"You got money to throw out on motel rooms?"

His nostrils tightened. "I got some."

"But Mrs. Douglas owes you more. How much?"

His eyes shifted.

"You hard of hearing? I asked how much Mrs. Douglas owed you."

A primitive hatred twisted his face for an instant. "A hunnert dollars."

A lie. The motel had to be costing at least forty-five. Would he have spent that much, gone to all this trouble for only a hundred?

"For what? Why does she owe you?"

"I buy stuff, for house."

"Come on—you spent a hundred dollars of your own on household stuff? You must think cops are dumb."

He pulled in smoke, his mouth drawn, his glance on a muddy maroon swirl in the carpeting.

"Felicia told us Mrs. Douglas promised you a bonus. What's the bonus for—something you did?"

"Iss wrong. I buy stuff."

She didn't believe him for a minute. "What kind of stuff?"

"I don't know—iss long time."

She caught Lawton's glance. His expression seemed to say *Let me have him—I'll make him talk*. She wasn't ready to do that.

She pulled out the picture of Sunmann, turned it so Garcia could see. "Know this man?"

The cigarillo dropped. He picked it up, laid it in an ashtray. "No."

"His name was Frankie Sunmann. He was killed the other night. He had the Douglas address and phone number in his pocket."

He put his hands in his pockets, stared past her at the wall.

"I think you and the man were connected. I think you did a fancy job on him."

"I don't do job! You *loco*, lady."

She had a sudden inspiration. "Okay, maybe you didn't shoot him. Maybe you gave Mrs. Douglas the gun, and that's what she owes you for."

"No!"

A line of sweat gleamed on his upper lip. He turned to get the towel, wiped his face. His eyes darted from her to Lawton and back again, calculating. "I do special job for Mees Douglas. Take package. She pay extra. *Mucho dinero*. Five hundred, she say she gonna give."

"She promised you five hundred bucks just to deliver a package? Where?"

He gestured toward the wall. "Here."

She leaned forward. "When was this?"

"Sunday."

The day before Sunmann had been killed—the day Douglas's boat had blown up.

"What kind of package?"

"*No sé.* Iss taped." With his hands he described a package as big as her purse. Could have had a gun in it.

She remembered something Denise had said; Garcia hadn't been working on Sunday. "I thought that was your day off."

For an instant he seemed flustered. "I come on day off. Mees Douglas ask special."

Was he telling the truth? When she'd questioned Bender and Kevin about whether "Amos Johnson" had had visitors, neither one had remembered any. "What time were you here?"

Garcia picked up the cigarillo again, took a drag. "'Bout three, four o'clock. I leave package. Then I go."

"Who'd she tell you to ask for?"

His glance sped to the wall, then back again. "She don' tell. She say leave package by door. Room *treinta y uno.*"

"And then what?"

"Ring bell and go away."

She looked at him skeptically. "You didn't hang around for a peek? Not even a quick one?"

His face seemed to narrow. His lips tightened.

"How long did you wait?"

"I go across street, stand behind building. In a while he open door."

"What'd he look like?"

"Big guy." He looked at Lawton, glanced away quickly. "Like him. Yellow hair." He pronounced it *jello.* "Eyes" —he pointed to hers.

"Blue?"

"*Sí.*"

A perfect description of Mitch Robler. She pulled out the snapshot Arden had given her. "This him?"

Garcia squinted at it uncertainly. "Maybe."

"But you're not sure."

"It look like the guy."

He was hedging. He didn't sound as though he recognized Robler.

"If it was such a hot package, why didn't Mrs. Douglas deliver it herself?"

"Mees Douglas home. Baby sick."

"How do you know if it was your day off?"

He tilted his head. "I know. She call, tell me come."

Cool customer. "And the next day, where was she then?"

His glance flitted to one side, then quickly back; trying to remember the truth or a carefully rehearsed lie? "Home. She stay in all day. Baby sick again."

That had been Monday. Arden herself had admitted that she'd gone to the motel on Monday, had had a fight with Robler.

Nikki wanted to be sure of his answer. "She was home all day?"

"Sí." He gave his full attention to the cigarillo, crushing it carefully, lighting another immediately. "Whole day, stay in."

"You were there, watching her?"

The line of sweat shone on his lip. "Sí."

He was lying.

"Got your green card on you?" she said. The card identified him as a legal alien. She hoped to throw him off balance; there was a hint of terror in his face as he dug it out of his wallet.

She pretended to study it, copied his alien registration number into her memo book just to add to his nervousness. Then, as she passed the card back, she snapped, "You're lying, Garcia. Know what happens when you talk bullshit to the cops?"

"Iss no bullshit—"

"The immigration people will be intersted in this. Think they'll let you bring your family here if you're in trouble with the cops—"

He closed the distance between them in an instant and grabbed her lapel. She felt her heart stop. She gripped her gun, feeling his hate like rancid fumes. "*Hijo de puta!* Child of a whore! I no lie!"

Behind her, she heard Lawton spring to his feet.

She met Garcia's stare. "Attacking a police officer is a crime in this country."

His hand dropped slowly to his side, but his jaw was hard, his eyes still blazing.

"Mrs. Douglas told me she came here Monday, Garcia. You're handing me a load of grade A garbage."

"She lie! She home with baby."

"You're the liar, mister. You put three bullets into Sunmann Monday night because Mrs. Douglas wanted you to, and now you're hanging around to collect for the job."

"Bitch woman!" he hissed.

"Watch that mouth, buddy." He subsided into heavy silence. She turned to Lawton. "We're wasting our time."

Garcia waited till they were out the door and a safe distance away, past the laundry room. Then he stuck his head out and blasted, "I don' kill this guy, ball breaker! *Guevona! Me cago en tu madre!* I shit on your mother!"

A string of curses followed them.

"Noisy bastard, isn't he?" Lawton remarked. "Think I'll go back and teach him some manners."

Ahead of them, the office door opened. Bender emerged and stared at them, horrified. His squiggle of mustache twitched.

"What's eating our friend the manager?" Lawton said. "He looks like he got his balls caught in the door."

Bender trotted forward, met them near the laundry

room. "Detective Trakos, I really can't have the police harassing our guests. I've a good mind to call your commander."

The thought of Bender complaining to Eagle-Eye made her sick. Eagle-Eye might think she needed even closer supervision.

She gave Bender a weak smile. "Can we talk?"

"Well—"

She tucked a hand under his elbow, guided him back to the office. Kevin, the sandy-haired clerk, had his head buried in a TV program as they passed.

The same ceramic fisherman was still trolling Bender's corn plant. She searched frantically for inspiration. "As a rule we don't tell civilians what's going on," she finally said, "but Mr. Garcia's pretty upset right now." She paused. "I mean, his mother. . . ."

Bender's eyes opened wide. "She was murdered?"

Lawton put in, "We're not really allowed. . . ."

Bender stroked his mustache with the tip of a knuckle. "Does this have anything to do with the other thing you came here about—that Amos Johnson?"

"Not really," Lawton said.

"You mean. . . ." His face seemed to collapse. "Why does everything happen to me?"

"While Mr. Garcia's here," Nikki said, "we need a record of his phone calls and visitors."

He frowned. "I don't know if my staff'll have the time—"

"I'd be so grateful." She widened her eyes, managed a smile.

"Kevin!" he called.

The boy slouched in, the points of his hair shadowing his face. Bender said, "I want you to keep an eye on anyone visiting Mr. Garcia. Note down any calls he makes, the time they come in, when he hangs up. Room nineteen. Got it?"

Kevin nodded and shuffled out.

"By the way," Nikki asked, "how long is Mr. Garcia registered for?"

"One night."

She handed him her card. "If he should check out suddenly, let me know."

She and Lawton ran through the drizzle toward the Fury. Lawton ducked behind the wheel, turned on the lights and windshield wipers.

She stared at the door of Garcia's room, the number 19 reflected in their headlights, the "9" missing a screw, hanging crookedly and hitting the "1." "Think he killed Sunmann?"

"Could've," Lawton said as he pulled out. "He's the kind who wouldn't give it a second thought. But why?"

"I haven't figured that out yet." A drop from her wet hair trickled down inside her collar. "Did he really see Johnson at the motel, or was that part of the line he was handing us?"

He turned onto Emmons, stopped for a light. "I don't know. I couldn't get his story straight."

She remembered the little man's masklike face, the terror in his eyes. "You know, I've seen scared guys in my time, but Garcia takes the prize."

Lawton seemed thoughtful. "If he didn't kill Sunmann, he probably knows who did." The light turned green, acid color reflecting on the wet asphalt. He squeezed down on the gas pedal and they moved ahead.

19

They ate at a steak house on Ocean Avenue. Free shrimp appetizer with every dinner order. Afterward Nikki found a phone and tried Marcia Breitson again. No one answered. She'd call again in the morning. If she still hadn't reached her, she'd run over to Robler's last address, question old neighbors, his landlord.

She dialed home, spoke to Lara. "How was school?"

"Okay."

"And dinner?"

"Okay. When'll you be home?"

She was about to say, "As soon as I can," when she remembered Lawton's advice. Don't clutch. "I don't know," she said. "I'll see you later."

It had been harder to do than she'd thought. She bit her lip, pressed her finger hard against the receiver cradle.

After a moment she dropped another coin into the slot, dialed the precinct. Two messages—the Professor and Kerrigan.

Kerrigan probably wanted to know when they'd return his gun. She dialed the Professor first.

A woman answered, her voice dry. "Yeah?"

"Sam Magliulo, please."

"Sam, it's for you."

She heard water running and a nearby phone ringing. It

was probably a counter shop, a bookmaker's operation run in a kitchen, the odds scribbled on a counter with a felt-tipped pen, easy to wipe off in case of a raid. She felt a momentary impulse to report the place, habit after her years in Public Morals.

"Hello," the Professor said after a short wait. "I have those prices you asked about." He couldn't talk freely.

"You get hold of the shys?" she said.

"Those are the ones."

"What's the story?"

"No trouble at all."

"He paid them?"

"Absolutely. By the week." His voice fell. "It's okay—I can talk now. Your guy Sunmann was as steady as a savings bank—no problem. You can't hang this one on the shys, Detective Trakos. They are bereft at his loss."

"Thanks, Professor. Come into the precinct and I'll—"

"There's something else." He paused. "It would require more research." Translation: More money. "But I think you'd be interested. I'm picking up signals of a larger incident in Brooklyn, something recent and important."

"What?"

"I can't be certain, but if you're interested, I can pursue the matter."

Something big had gone down, something tied to organized crime, maybe. She racked her brain for gangland-style executions, major holdups, could think of nothing. "Find out."

"I think you've made a wise decision." His voice got louder. "Those are the best prices I can quote you. Let me know how many you want." The line went dead.

She dropped another coin in the phone slot, tried Kerrigan. His voice blasted over the wire. "I can't reach her! Arden said she left for school this morning, and—"

"Wait a minute—slow down. Who left—Denise?"

"Who the hell else? That bitch is lying! Denise wouldn't take off without saying good-bye."

"Maybe she tried to call—"

"That's shit! I just talked to her this morning. Why didn't she say anything to me then? She—"

"Mr. Kerrigan, how can I help you?"

"Get over there and search the place."

"You want to put in a complaint?"

"Isn't that what I'm doing?"

"No—you have to go down to the precinct and report her missing—"

"You kidding? I'm gonna waste time watching them fill out a bunch of forms?" He snorted. "I should've known better than to call the cops. Bunch of candy-asses. You fucked me good at my job. That prick Madden's watching me like a hawk—wants to know what kind of trouble I'm in."

"Listen, we just—"

The line went dead.

She hung up. "Kerrigan's wild," she said to Lawton.

"So what else is new?"

"I wanted to tell him his gun's clean, but he didn't give me a chance. He hasn't been able to reach Denise since this morning. He thinks something happened to her, and he wants me to organize a search." Kerrigan was a nut job, but as she spoke to Lawton she was troubled. Kerrigan knew Denise as well as anyone. If she'd stepped out of her ordinary pattern, maybe there was reason to worry.

Why was she letting herself get hooked by Denise Douglas? She had enough on her plate with Sunmann's murder. Days had gone by since he'd died and all they had were bits and pieces, hints, trails.

With an effort, she pulled her thoughts off the girl and went to the car. They had a nine o'clock date to meet Arnold Greenberg, go through a rerun on his final evening with his friend Frankie Sunmann. With any luck, maybe it would yield something solid. If it did, she could bargain with Eagle-Eye for more time.

"This is exactly where we sat, in this booth," Greenberg said, pointing to the black Formica table. It was identical to the dozen others around them in the Golden Knish. Nikki watched the counterman slice a side of corned beef, layer a thick sandwich between two pieces of rye, wipe chunky red hands on his apron, and set the plate atop the glass counter. The waiter delivered it and Greenberg demolished the first half with two quick bites. "This is what I ate—exactly." A drop of mustard fell on the soft balloon of his chin and he wiped it away with pudgy fingers. "The trouble is it's not helping me remember anything new about Sunday night."

"Something may come back to you," Lawton said. "You never know what'll connect."

"I really want to help"—he chomped off a piece of pickle— "but my mind's a blank."

He finished the sandwich and they paid the check. Greenberg bought a jumbo-size bag of corn chips on the way out. He tucked himself behind the wheel of his car, offered the bag around, then placed it between Lawton and himself. Nikki sat in the back, facing Greenberg's neck; it squeezed over his collar like pink dough overflowing a bowl.

Lawton said, "Okay. Do just what you did Sunday."

"When I took Frankie home?"

"Right."

"Well, I got onto Avenue U."

"Show me."

Greenberg shrugged. "Okay, if you want." He pulled out, merged with traffic. "I don't care, but it's just straight driving. I mean, we went down U—" He stopped suddenly. In the mirror Nikki saw his eyes snap wide open, like a doll's. He pulled over to the curb.

"What's the matter?" Lawton said.

"I just thought of something. Frankie had to pee. We went along on U, and here we are in the middle of nowhere, no gas stations, no bars, and he has to go." He crunched a corn chip. "We went back to the restaurant, but they were locked up by then, and they didn't want to open just so he could use the john. I asked Frankie couldn't he wait till he got home, but he had this crazy thing—once he had the urge he couldn't hold it. So I said I'd take him a few blocks over and he could get out and go in the bushes."

"Where?" Lawton asked.

"I'll show you."

He started the car again, drove a short distance. The rows of small brick houses ended abruptly. The land became flat and marshy. He pulled onto the shoulder of the road, next to a stand of waist-high reeds, and they got out. Cars cruised by, lighting up the small group. Drivers craned around curiously.

"He went in the bushes," Greenberg said.

Nikki and Lawton walked back and forth pushing the reeds aside. "There's a path here," Nikki said. A narrow track led downward.

Greenberg went back to the car to wait while they walked down the path. Nikki's heels sank deep into the soft loam. For a brief moment she thought of the layer of mud collecting on the expensive suede, then forgot it and focused on keeping her balance.

Except for the occasional *whoosh* of cars rushing by above, it was completely quiet. They came out into a marina, mostly empty now that winter was approaching. A few boats rocked in the hushed slips under dim security lights. They pushed through the loam toward a ramp between the slips, climbed up a clanking steel catwalk. The sign on the building above read, SAFE HARBOR MARINA.

Lawton looked at the rotted coils of nautical line, rusted motor parts, cinder blocks. "Nothing here."

"Not now. But maybe Sunmann saw something on Sunday."

They clanked down the walkway. It was as they moved through the slips that she noticed the boat, a fair-sized cabin cruiser on the end. Even in the patchy light the letters *Flora* stood out boldly.

Her heart thudded against her ribs. "That's the boat that helped the Coast Guard search for Douglas."

She walked down the wooden ramp and hoisted herself over the side rail, Lawton right behind her. She unbuttoned the grommets holding the protective canvas.

"What're you looking for?"

She peered into the shadows. "I'm not sure."

A lock gleamed on the undercabin door. The upper cabin seemed whistle clean. She moved forward and slid behind the wheel, faced the control panel. Her glance fell on a drawer under the teak and she pulled it open. Three pieces of paper, a clip, two rubber bands. "Got a flashlight?" she said.

Lawton pulled a book of matches out of his pocket, lit one and held it over the drawer. By the flickering light she made out a tide table, a list of emergency instructions, a registration form. She was about to read the name on the form when the match went out. Lawton lit another.

"It's registered to John Leucometti," she said. "The name mean anything to you?"

"Are you kidding? Leucometti's a lieutenant in the Calabese mob—this boat belongs to Family."

"Mafia? Wait a minute—it's beginning to make sense. The *Flora* is the boat that helps the Coast Guard search for Douglas, right? Good Samaritan, and all that. But who's to say the *Flora* hasn't just blown Douglas to hell? They hide an explosive on board Douglas's boat, come within range of him, and set it off with a detonating device."

"A contract?"

"That's right—a hit. Paid for by Arden and lover boy. My stoolie just told me something big went down in Brooklyn recently. Maybe it's this—the timing's good. The boat blew up about seven. This was two, three hours later."

"It feels right."

"So they're coming in, and now Sunmann's down here. He sees something. Maybe they're carrying off equipment or something—I'm not sure what."

"So? Why should Sunmann care *what* they're carrying?"

"I don't know yet." What was bothering her about Sunmann, teasing her brain, demanding attention? She almost had it, but not quite.

They rebuttoned the grommets, careful to leave the *Flora* exactly as they'd found it, and climbed onto the wooden ramp again. They passed through the swaying slips and found the path. One of her heels felt wobbly and she placed her feet carefully, putting most of her weight on her toes.

At the base of the rise she scooped a handful of mud into a plastic evidence bag. "I'm still looking for the gook on Sunmann's shoes," she said.

"You want it analyzed fast, give it to me. One of the lab guys owes me."

When they got to the car Greenberg was eating the last corn chip.

Nikki said, "I need to know when you got here Sunday. As close as you can figure it."

He poked into the corners of the bag, searching for crumbs. "About ten-ten, ten-fifteen. The deli closes at ten. We were the last ones in there, and by the time we went back to see if we could use the john and then came here it must've been ten, fifteen minutes."

Overhead, an airplane dipped on its approach to Kennedy. "What was Frankie's mood on the way home?" she asked.

"The way he always was. Nothing special."

Then whatever had excited Sunmann had happened afterward—after Greenberg had dropped him off. His landlord said he'd come running down a half hour later "all excited" and asked for the phone directory. What could have sparked him at that hour? She pictured Sunmann alone in his sparely furnished room. No one had phoned, he'd received no mail on Monday.

She pointed toward the reeds. "Was he down there long?" she asked Greenberg.

"A while—maybe five minutes. I guess he was smoking. He didn't smoke in front of me—he was trying to stop and I made him put them out when I caught him. So he'd sneak one whenever he could. When he came back up I smelled smoke all over him. I said, 'Frankie, you had a cig, didn't you?' But he said, 'Are you nuts?' "

Arnold's eyes squeezed down suddenly inside the thick folds of flesh. He pulled out a handkerchief and wiped away the tears. "Isn't it funny, all that fighting about the cigarettes, and in the end it didn't matter a damn. I feel like telling him that. If I could have him back, I'd say, 'I'm sorry, Frankie. Smoke all the cigs you want.' "

20

Nikki and Lawton sat in the Fury and watched Greenberg pull away. Her mind drifted back to Kerrigan's frantic phone call. She wondered if Denise had turned up yet.

"I'm worried about the Douglas girl," she said. "It strikes me Kerrigan was telling the truth—she wouldn't go away without letting him know. She's careful around him."

"Want to go talk to the widow?"

"I think so."

He started the motor. "You got it."

A fine drizzle dotted the windshield, turned into a steady flow by the time they parked. They hurried up the path to the Douglas place, almost ran into Rick Kerrigan, barreling toward them from the door.

Lawton held him off with a hand. "Hey, watch it!"

"Oh, it's you!" He was bareheaded, the collar of his jacket pulled up. "You took your sweet time. Denise isn't here. That bitch Arden showed me how her room's cleaned out and all her stuff's gone." He tossed his head to shake water off his hair, his eyes narrow and dangerous. "She says she went to school early. To get away from *me* —you believe that shit?"

Nikki could believe it, wondered what had attracted the girl to him in the first place. Rain was pelting the back of her legs, soaking her feet in the open sandals. She started toward the door and Lawton followed, but Kerrigan was right behind. His voice was loud, belligerent.

"Denise never did that before. She *wouldn't*. Fucking Arden told me she's staying with a friend. She said Denise wouldn't tell her the name in case I went after her. But I called all her friends—no one heard from her. So that's crap!"

Lawton rang the bell. "Why don't you go home? Maybe she'll call you."

Kerrigan didn't seem to hear. "I'm gonna go to her dorm and look under every bed, turn the place upside down. If I don't find her, I'll come back here and tear the fucking house apart."

Lawton put a hand on his sleeve. "Take it easy, buddy."

Kerrigan brushed his hand away, eyes blazing. "I don't need a fucking father. When do I get my gun back?"

"It's still at the lab," Nikki put in quickly. It was in the glove compartment of the Fury, but she wasn't about to hand a gun to a lunatic. Let him cool down first.

"Thanks a lot! You been a great help, lady." He hunched into his jacket and ran toward the street.

Lawton leaned on the buzzer again. "Nasty bastard. Looking for trouble."

Nikki shivered as a gust of wind hit her. "Arden's taking a long time."

"Yeah, where'd she disappear to?"

Arden seemed weary when she opened the door, pale and drawn under her tan. Barefoot, she wore a figured silk kimono, its belt loose around her waist. Her hair was tied back, auburn strands escaping from a velvet ribbon. She shivered inside the kimono as the damp, cold air hit her but didn't ask them in. "Oh. Isn't it kind of late?"

Nikki leaned toward the door to escape a drip from the overhang. "We have some questions."

"This isn't a good time."

She was trying to hold the door open only a crack, but the wind took it. In the moment before she grabbed it again Nikki glimpsed a scene of total disorder. The floor was littered with bright blocks, a paper bag stuffed with what looked like rags, loose sheets of newspaper, a heap of dirty laundry. A child's overalls had come loose from the pile, turquoise straps dragging on the marble next to the tub of decaying roses. Nikki couldn't help remembering the first time she'd come to the house, when the uniformed maid had answered and it had looked like a Hollywood set.

The dampness was starting to chill her to the bone. Why was Arden keeping them out? "Can we come in?"

"I don't feel well."

"I'm sorry. It'll only take a minute."

"No—I don't feel up to it. Denise's crazy boyfriend just left."

"Mrs. Douglas, he seems to think something's wrong—"

"Oh, please! Why does he keep hounding me? I *told* him what happened. If he won't believe it, that's not my problem."

"What did happen?" A splash of rain missed Nikki's nose by a hair, landed on her exposed toe.

"Denise got sick of him, that's what. He's no good. Barry had him investigated right before he died. Denise thought he'd given up drugs, but he's still dealing—over in Bensonhurst, where he lives. He's got a going business—crack, heroin, the works. Well, I told her about it and she decided she'd be better off without him."

"She just left? Without saying anything—"

"She was scared to tell him to his face."

"He tried reaching her at friends—"

"She wouldn't even tell *me* where she was going. She said he'd trail her there and make her life miserable."

"But if she said—"

"She said, he said! I'm sick of being in the middle of it! Haven't I had enough, losing my husband the way I did? Everyone seems to forget it was less than a week ago." In the middle of her Poor Bereaved Widow role she caught Nikki's glance and looked away, as though she'd just remembered she'd told her about the affair with Robler. She tugged on the belt of the robe. "I've got a blinding headache. Can we cut this short?"

Not if Nikki could help it. "Just one favor. Can I use your bathroom?"

Something changed in the depths of Arden's eyes. Nikki could sense her reluctance. After a moment's hesitation she stepped aside, pointed toward the hallway leading to the library. "On your left."

Nikki glanced sideways at Lawton, slipped inside the house. The hallway was as messy as the entry. More toys, a child's sneaker mixed in. On the floor of the cocoa and gold bathroom, towels in a damp heap near a corner piled with clothing. The house had an eerie feel to it—the mess and the deep quiet.

Nikki left the bathroom, tiptoed across to the library. On the glass coffee table the remains of a takeout meal, white cardboard containers and paper cups. Impossible to tell how many people had eaten, but it looked like more than one. Books off the shelves, in large and small piles all over the floor and every usable surface.

In spite of the clutter, the room seemed to be missing something. What? Then she saw it; the desk was heaped with books—the picture of Barry Douglas was gone.

Two suitcases stood behind the sofa. She lifted them. Heavy. Packed and strapped but not labeled. She remembered the airline ticket Denise had seen. Arden was leaving tomorrow.

She wanted to go through the desk drawers, but she'd

taken more than enough time. Arden would begin to wonder, might come looking for her. She headed back.

She stepped under the chandelier, heard Lawton ask, "Your housekeeper been here?"

"Ramon? Not since yesterday." She turned as Nikki's heels sounded on the entry floor. "I hope we're through."

"That's it," Nikki said. "Good night, Mrs. Douglas."

They walked down the path. The door thunked shut behind them.

Lawton took out the car keys. "So what was all that about? A waste of time."

"Not really. There's something strange going down in that place. Looks like it got hit by a tornado."

He turned up Coney Island Avenue, drove under the parkway structure, slowed at U as a car cut them off to go to Burger King. "Didn't you say she was going away?"

"Sure, but what about the maids? She let them *all* go? It's weird. She isn't the kind to live in a mess like that. She's fussy about herself, how everything looks." She tapped on the armrest. "We're supposed to be working on Sunmann," she said. "Why do I keep coming back to Arden Douglas?"

"What was she saying about the wild man?"

"Kerrigan?"

"Yeah—that he was free-lancing drugs. Thought I knew all the dealers in Brooklyn. He's a new one."

She held the side strap as they turned onto Foster. "Maybe you didn't pick him up."

"Doubt it. My connections are real good. Tell you something. I've been thinking about him. Most dealers are junkies—this kid doesn't look like one. Steady job, nice girlfriend—"

"But he *could* be. He had that trouble in school."

"Yeah," he said thoughtfully. "He could be."

He pulled into her driveway.

"Coffee?" he asked.

"Don't you ever give up?"

"No."

She looked out at the maple leaves shadowing the hood. "The case has me swallowed up," she warned him. "I can't focus on anything else."

He met her glance directly. "If I said all I wanted was coffee, I'd be lying." He shut off the motor. "But I'm willing to settle for that."

As long as they understood one another.

He followed her up the steps. Lara was nowhere in sight. In bed, probably. Was she sleeping or waiting for Nikki to come in?

Mrs. Binsey was watching a rerun of an old Bette Davis movie. "Did you have any trouble?" Nikki asked.

Mrs. Binsey looked up, confused for a moment. "With Lara? Oh, no, she never gives me trouble."

What did that mean? Was Lara finally accepting Nikki's crazy hours? Or was Mrs. Binsey her usual insensitive self?

Lawton waited while she paid the sitter, leaned against the kitchen doorway while she set up the coffee maker. Even now she found herself drifting back to the Sunmann case. She'd been honest with Lawton; her mind was full of unresolved facts gathered over the past two days. Momentarily she felt guilt toward her mother. *I need to focus on my work, not the guy, Mom. I can't help it.* Her mother, more old-fashioned than her father, had been broken-hearted when she'd joined the force, had slowly resigned herself to Nikki's career. "She should have found a man," her mother had said. "That is a woman's destiny."

"That is the Greek way," her father had argued. "The American way is better. Let her know the world, be a person for herself."

At times like this she felt taken over by her profession, as though she had no other identity besides cop.

Kerrigan had been a drug dealer. Where there were drugs, other crimes followed.

She held the coffee filter in midair. "Didn't Kerrigan live in Bensonhurst?"

"Yeah."

"So did Sunmann."

He wandered into the hallway while she set water to boil for her tea. He stood before a picture taken years ago, showing Nikki and her father on the boat with a crowd of customers. "How old were you here?"

She came out and squinted at the skinny kid in oilskins, already taller than all the men aboard. "Fifteen."

She went back into the kitchen, took two mugs from the cabinet. "If Kerrigan pushed—"

"We only have the widow's word for it."

"Maybe he sold to Sunmann. I found some stuff in his room."

"Pot." He came in and sat down at the table, tilted the chair back on two legs. "If Sunmann had a stronger habit, he kept it under wraps."

"Maybe he did. Maybe his brother doesn't know everything he did in Vietnam."

"Maybe." He tapped the chair lightly with his index finger. "Depends on whether the widow's telling the truth, and whether Sunmann even knew this character. Anyhow, his gun's clean."

"I know. But I was just thinking—what if he had another thirty-eight, an unregistered one? That would put him back in the picture." She handed him a mug of coffee, shook her head. "Too many unknowns. When a case comes together, it seems to slide into place easy, not like this. I'll see what else I can dig up on Kerrigan, talk to his mother, maybe."

"Aunt Nikki. . . ." Lara's thin voice called from the bedroom.

"Uh-oh." Nikki stood up. "Be back in a minute."

"I'd like to meet her."

She hesitated, surprised. "Okay, I'll ask."

She turned on Lara's bedside lamp. Her small face was shadowed by the cloud of bright hair. "You didn't come in to say good night." She looked worried.

"I have company. Can he say hello?"

Her answer was so low Nikki made her repeat it. "Okay."

She led Lawton in, feeling edgy. Would they like each other? Why did that seem important?

"Lara, this is Detective Lawton. My niece, Lara."

"Hello," Lawton said.

Lara mumbled something that was lost in her hair. Nikki's heart went out to her. She looked so small and lonely in the big bed. Since the Sunmann case Nikki had hardly spent any time with her. It had been only three days—it felt more like three weeks.

"Your aunt tells me you like ships," Lawton said.

Lara was silent. Maybe it had been a bad idea letting him come in, too upsetting for Lara at bedtime.

"There's her collection." Nikki showed him the shelf. "My father made most of them."

He admired the Spanish galleon, the whaler, the pilot boat, then turned back to Lara. "I make boats, too."

Lara sat up straighter, eyed him.

"Got a piece of paper?" he asked.

"What kind?"

"Any kind." He held his hands out, palms facing. "About this big."

She found a piece of construction paper in her desk, handed it to him. Nikki watched in fascination as he folded, bent, turned the sheet. A tiny boat formed under his fingers, its hull square and trim, its sail lifting jauntily.

"That's origami, the Japanese art of folding paper." He looked at Nikki. "I learned it from my partner on a three-day stakeout."

Lara couldn't take her eyes off the boat.

"Want it?" he asked.

She looked at him. Nikki realized how unused to men Lara was. She'd never known a father, had no uncles. Nikki's father was the only man she was close to, and that was for two months a year, on summer vacations.

Lawton held out the boat. "Keep it—it's your paper, right?"

"Okay."

He put it up on the shelf next to the schooner Nikki had won in Coney Island. She said good night to Lara, tucked her under the quilt. Her niece's arms reached up suddenly, circled Nikki's neck. She clung so hard Nikki had to unwind her arms to straighten. Maybe she shouldn't have sprung a surprise like that on Lara. She wasn't used to new people, wasn't comfortable with them.

When they got back to the kitchen Lawton said, "My kid looked like that when she was little."

"You miss her?"

"Yeah." He took a sip of coffee, set down the mug. "Cold."

"I'll get you another cup."

"Don't—it's late. Let's call it a night." He slipped on his coat.

She walked him to the door. For a moment she thought he would kiss her, but instead he touched her cheek gently with warm fingertips, then ran down the steps. "Talk to you tomorrow," he called.

She went to bed, tossed restlessly, thought about the case. She heard her mother's voice dimly, *You're so buried in your work you'll never find a man. What's wrong with you, Nikoula mou?* Was her mother right? Would she never stand before the altar while the best man exchanged the couple's crowns three times? Would she never see her father, bursting with pride, lead the *tsamiko*, circling and weaving among the tables while the wedding guests ate, smashed plates and threw money?

For a moment she wondered whether she should have tried to pay more attention to Lawton. But at this stage of the case it was hopeless. She had the feeling the Sunmann murder was solvable—why wasn't she putting it together right?

The bright green numbers on the digital alarm glowed eerily. One-fifteen. Two-thirty. Three-oh-five.

The next thing she knew, light was seeping through the blinds. Six-fifty.

She heard water running in the bathroom next door, noises through the wall. She sat up, fully awake. Lara never woke up earlier than she. It usually took a derrick to get her out of bed.

Maybe she was sick. Maybe after last night's surprise guest Lara had a monumental stomachache.

She sprang out of bed, knocked on the bathroom door. "You all right?"

"Yes."

Her niece came out of the bathroom fully dressed. Nikki tried to keep her mouth from dropping open. "Is there a special reason you have to be at school early?"

"No."

Nikki showered and changed, walked into the kitchen. Lara had filled two bowls with corn flakes, had made tea for Nikki, and poured a glass of milk for herself. Nikki was delighted, afraid to spoil it by saying anything.

Lara finished her corn flakes. "He really is a cop, isn't he?" she said abruptly, her tone offhand.

"That's right."

She gulped down the milk, grabbed her books and jacket. "See you tonight."

She ran down the steps and Nikki heard the front door slam. She went into Lara's room and watched from the window as her niece ran between the leaves, then disappeared around the corner. It was then that she realized Lara had forgotten to kiss her good-bye. A slip? Or had she *meant* to forget?

She turned away from the window. Her glance fell on the shelf holding the ship collection. The schooner stood next to the models her father had made, but Lawton's paper boat was missing.

She looked around the room but didn't see it anywhere.

Nikki got to the office early.

The Professor's was the first call that came in for her. "I have some information for you, Nikki. We're talking high-level arson. But not a torching."

"A boat explosion?"

"Exactly. Barry Douglas is the name. Rumor has it the customer paid a significant price."

"Who ordered it?"

"Don't know, but I'll keep asking." She heard a click as the connection was broken.

Something eased in her—she was headed in the right direction. None of it made sense yet, but at least she hadn't been spinning her wheels.

A boat explosion—ordered by Arden? The average woman didn't have direct links to organized crime. Maybe Arden's boyfriend, Mitch Robler, had ordered the hit. Anyhow, who said Arden was the average woman?

She should try to locate Mitch Robler, trace him through his last known address if she couldn't reach Marcia

Breitson. She took out her memo book, stared at the scribbled notations, wondered why she couldn't get going. Something troubled her, just out of reach, kept whispering that she was wasting time following the obvious leads on this one.

She poured herself a cup of tea. The phone rang. It was Lawton. "Bingo on the mud sample," he said. "Matches the gook on Sunmann's shoes exactly."

"Then we're right—Sunmann was down at the marina. I just talked to my stoolie. Douglas was set up, a professional job."

"Who bought it?"

"He doesn't know yet."

"So now you really have to turn this Douglas stuff over."

"It's just beginning to tie up. Sunmann must've seen the *Flora* come in. And he must've seen something else, something worth bucks."

"Yeah, like what—a wise guy carrying a stick of dynamite? The pros are smarter than that. Think about it." He paused. "Listen, this duffel bag case is starting to break. They brought the guy in and he's making a statement. Going to be hard to reach me."

"Okay. Call me when you're free."

She hung up and walked to the window. Two cars had stopped in the middle of Coney Island Avenue. The driver of the first, a Hasidic Jew with dark beard, curly sideburns, and yarmulke, walked menacingly toward the young black man who sat in the second car. The bearded driver shouted that he'd been cut off. Horns blared as traffic began to back up. Two cops going out on the early tour waded into the center of it, persuaded the bearded man back into his car, and broke it up.

Nikki stayed at the window, staring at cars and pedestrians. Lawton was right, of course. If she couldn't see the link between Douglas and Sunmann, she should give it over. Right away. Ernie Doblinski at Coast Guard head-quarters would know who should get it. She reached for the phone, then slowly pulled her hand away.

One last look at everything wouldn't hurt.

She pulled out all the reports she'd sent or received in the three days since Sunmann had been found, reread them. Then she looked at the pile of evidence bags, turned each one over. A case broke when some energetic detective asked the right question, one that had never been asked before. What should she ask? She looked at the pile on her desk. Trivial bits of evidence—nothing important here. Maybe if she followed Lawton's advice and separated the two cases, she'd be able to focus more clearly on Sunmann, find his killer.

She had a depressing thought—maybe *Eagle-Eye* had been on target when he'd tried to take the homicide away. She was too inexperienced to know what to ask, how to put the case together. She should have let him replace her right away.

The black match folder from the Three Bears Restaurant caught her eye. She remembered finding it in Sunmann's room, thinking how out of place it seemed. Suddenly Arnold Greenberg's words came back to her— "When he came back up I smelled smoke all over him. I said, 'Frankie, you had a cig, didn't you?' "

Sunmann had had a cigarette lighter in his pocket when he'd died—but it hadn't worked.

The address of the Three Bears Restaurant was em-bossed in a corner of the match folder: 76 Pine Street, in the financial district. Douglas had worked nearby. She copied the address into her memo book.

She *had* thought of a question to ask, but it was a wild one, based on a way-out theory. If she took her new idea seriously, it gave her a totally different view of the Sunmann case—and of Douglas's murder, too. But could she believe in it?

Suddenly excited, she stuffed the papers and plastic bags back into her drawer and ran down to the Fury.

Pine was a narrow street threading through the financial district, so shadowed that when Nikki turned into it she felt night had suddenly fallen. The darkness was partly from the skyscrapers that loomed over it, partly from scaffolding between the buildings that extended for several blocks. Near Water Street it got lighter and she found the Three Bears, a prosperous-looking establishment, windows framed in natural oak, velveteen curtains hung from brass rings.

The doors of the restaurant were locked, though there were lights behind the frosted glass. She rapped against the wood. A burly Asian man appeared and waved her away. They weren't open to customers. She held her ID where he could see it. The latch clicked as the door was unlocked.

The interior was dark and swank—the kind of place where deals were made and bragged about. It was being set up for the day's business. A barman polished glasses and placed them carefully in an overhead rack. A woman pushed a vacuum across the carpeting.

The Asian man introduced himself as Johnny Kim, the manager, and led her to a quiet corner. He was dark-skinned, with sharp eyes behind large silver-rimmed glasses, and a full, generous mouth.

He didn't recognize Sunmann's face from the photo.

She put the picture away. "Did Barry Douglas ever come in here?"

"The guy who was killed this week? Sure. Almost every day."

"You sure this man Sunmann wasn't with him?"

"No, never. I mostly saw Mr. Douglas with business types, cooking deals. That was at lunch." He winked at her. "After hours, his tastes ran different."

"Women?"

"One in particular—just lately." He pushed his glasses up his nose. "See, he always stopped in for a drink after work. At four-thirty—you could set your watch by it. A while ago—maybe two, three months—he started coming down a lot later—a good hour or two after everyone else was gone. About seven." His eyes were alert behind the thick lenses. "She was a cute-looking trick. They'd stop on the corner, he'd put her in a cab, then he'd come in here for a quickie. Two, three times a week. Always the same woman."

"What'd she look like?"

"Young. Dark and pretty. Very tiny—maybe five feet, no more. Her hair real short."

He opened his palms and gestured around his head to indicate the style. Nikki had a sudden recollection of Felicia Garcia's dark hair falling in twin wings toward her cheeks. "Thanks, Mr. Kim," she said. "You've been very helpful."

21

The elevator rose to twenty-three, the executive floor of
the Douglas, Roth building. Nikki tried to absorb what
she'd learned at the Three Bears, found her brain reject-
ing the information like foreign tissue. Barry Douglas
having an affair? She remembered his insurance broker's
words—"he was nuts about his wife." And what was it
Denise had said about her father and Arden? "He thought
she was a princess. If she sneezed, he'd run for a tissue."
Still . . .

Maybe it wasn't an affair. It could have something to
do with the ten million dollars. How much did Felicia
know about what Douglas was doing?

The doors opened on twenty-three. The pale blonde
receptionist remembered her.

"Is Mr. Douglas's secretary in today?"

"Ms. Garcia? Yes. She's at her desk."

When Nikki had spoken to Felicia in the Bronx she
hadn't mentioned that she'd been Douglas's secretary.
Come to think of it, she'd left out quite a bit.

She passed reception and turned a corner, saw a
luxuriously furnished room in the shape of an oval, doors
leading off into executive offices. The sofas and lounge
chairs were done in beiges and grays, subtle shades that
made it look like a living room. It was hard to imagine
anyone working here.

Felicia sat alone at the near end of the oval, hunched into a tense ball, punching numbers into a phone. The black wings of patent-leather hair hid her face.

She turned, saw Nikki, and froze, dropping the receiver. "What're you doing here?" she whispered. "What do you want?"

"Why didn't you say you were Douglas's secretary?"

"What has that got to do with anything?"

"I don't know. You tell *me*. How was Sunmann mixed up with Douglas?"

The receiver dangled off the desk, hanging by its wire. She picked it up, set it back into the cradle. "How should I know?"

"I think you *do*. You were more than just a secretary to Douglas—"

"What do you mean?"

"You were seen leaving with him two, three times a week—late at night, after everyone was gone."

Her lips drew into a straight line. "Someone has a big mouth." She stood, gave her chair a sharp push so that it caromed away from the desk. "That was work—we were busy."

"Not according to his wife. She said he hadn't worked late in months. Miss Garcia, if you know something, it isn't always smart to keep it from the cops."

The dark eyes peeked from beneath the veil of hair. For the first time she looked vulnerable, frightened. She looked like a kid—how old could she be?

Nikki softened her tone. "Maybe we can help you—or your father."

Felicia's lip trembled. Then the phone rang. Her eyes lit with hope, and she grabbed for it. Her expression changed to disappointment as she listened. "*Sí*," she said in a tired voice. She reached for the cross that hung on her cashmere sweater, slid it back and forth on its chain.

"*Sí.*" From her desk drawer she pulled a list of figures, read them off in Spanish. "I'll bring the chart over," she said into the phone.

Nikki waited till she'd replaced the receiver. "You speak Spanish on the job?"

"That's right. Barry hired me because I'm bilingual. He—he didn't speak it at all."

Nikki had the feeling she'd wanted to add something but had changed her mind.

She folded the list of figures, pulled an envelope from the drawer.

"Ms. Garcia, what do you know about Frankie Sunmann?"

"I told you already—nothing! Ask me a hundred times— there isn't any more. I swear!" Her voice wavered. "I have to work and I can't even think straight!" She inserted the paper into an envelope. Her fingers trembled. It took two tries.

"It's your father you're trying to protect, isn't it? What did he tell you?"

Felicia's finger slid along the envelope flap and the paper nicked the fleshy tip. She snatched it back and sucked on the cut.

"Why are you making it so hard on yourself?"

Her face was white and pinched. She looked weary, as though she were carrying a heavy load, looking for a place to rest it.

"I can help you," Nikki said.

For a moment Nikki thought she was going to break down, but she stiffened and said, "Excuse me." Then she turned and fled toward reception.

Keeping her eye on an older woman across the oval, Nikki went through Felicia's desk. There was a business letter in Spanish with a typed translation attached to it. Felicia had signed, "Translated by F. Garcia."

In the bottom drawer she found a Spanish-English

dictionary that reminded her of the one she'd seen in Douglas's library, a current issue of a fashion magazine, a pair of pantyhose in a plastic egg.

She waited five minutes for Felicia to return, then went to find her.

She moved back toward reception, sighted her in a small cubicle just beyond the elevator, past the plate glass doors. She was holding a phone, listening again. Even at this distance Nikki could see the white of her fingers as she gripped the receiver. Her free hand raked through her hair and separated the strands, making it look wild and unkempt. Why hadn't she gone back to her own desk to use the phone?

Nikki slipped past the plate glass doors and came up behind her. She asked softly, "Who is it you keep trying to reach?"

Felicia whirled around and put a knuckle in her mouth.

"You might as well tell me. I can have the call traced," Nikki said, not knowing whether she could or not.

"It's—my father." She swallowed. "He told me . . . When he talked to me last night he was okay. He said he was coming home first thing this morning. I keep calling home, but he's not there." Her voice rose, held an edge of panic. "I don't even know where to reach him."

"I do. We saw him last night at a motel in Brooklyn."

"Where?" She looked as though Nikki had handed her a miracle. "Oh, tell me. Please."

"First I need to know some things. What did he say to you—why was Mrs. Douglas going to give him money?"

Felicia bit her lip. "He said he had a chance to make it big. That she *had* to pay him. He said he knew enough to send them both to jail for a long time."

"Mrs. Douglas?"

She nodded, eyes wide and dark.

"And who else?"

"He wouldn't tell me. He said I was better off not knowing." She wrung her hands together. "He was supposed to get the money last night. And then come home today. Early. Please, if you know where he is, call him."

"One more thing. You were Douglas's secretary. Did you help him with his scam—the ten million dollars?"

"Are you crazy? I found out when everyone else did. Barry did that one all by himself."

Nikki had expected her to deny it, but for some reason she believed her. Felicia was shrewd, but Douglas was a smooth operator. He might have kept it from her.

Felicia picked up the receiver, dialed "9" and handed her the phone. "*Please.* See if you can reach my father."

Nikki dialed the motel. "Star Garden," a bored voice answered.

"Kevin? This is Detective Trakos." She heard a TV playing in the background, pictured the boy gazing at the screen hypnotized. "Let me speak to Mr. Garcia."

"Uh-uh. He called last night, said he didn't want to be disturbed."

"Listen, Kevin, I want to disturb him. Ring the phone."

"Well, I—"

"Go ahead. I'll take responsibility."

"Just a minute."

She waited while he chewed gum noisily in her ear. After a minute he said, "He doesn't answer."

She felt her stomach knot. Maybe Garcia was in the shower. "I'll hold on. Go open the door."

"Uh-uh. Can't do that. Chambermaid's got the spare keys on the rented rooms. She doesn't get here for another half hour."

She put the phone back into the cradle slowly. Felicia looked stricken.

"It's probably nothing," Nikki said. "He asked not to be disturbed. He might've changed his mind about leaving

early, decided to sleep a little later." Felicia's skin was
eggshell color, like the walls.

Nikki called the precinct, explained the situation to
Mantell, asked him to send a car to the motel. "I can't do
that, Trakos. The guys are all out on a ten-thirteen."
Ten-thirteen was the code signal for "assist patrolman."
An officer needed immediate backup; every available car
would respond. "I'll put it down for when someone's
free."

She hung up, turned to Felicia. "I'm going out there."

"Take me with you—please. I can't work—all I can
think of is how he is, whether he's all right."

"Okay, get your coat."

Felicia was back in seconds, racing to press the elevator
button, pushing it with her open palm. Out on the street,
she ran alongside Nikki, trotting to keep up with her long
stride as they rushed toward the Fury. "Maybe he went to
get the newspaper," Felicia said hopefully, "and that's
why he didn't answer the phone."

"Maybe," Nikki said, though she didn't believe it.

The FBI light lay on the floor of the front seat. She
pulled it out and pitched it up so its magnet caught on
the roof, plugged the wire into the dashboard lighter.
The revolving red light came on. She flicked on the siren,
tore into traffic.

She maneuvered through lower Manhattan. Even with
the siren squawking, some cars made way for her slug-
gishly. On the Bowery she almost lost her cool with one
driver, a swarthy young man with badly cratered skin,
who had her practically riding his bumper. Son of a
bitch, if I had the time, I'd take your number and ticket
you. What if this were an ambulance, and I had a dying
patient—would you move your ass then? New York drivers!
The same jerks who made you want to climb walls com-

plained the loudest about police response time—"The cops took all day to get there." A gap opened on Crater Face's right and she climbed through and got away from him.

She sped across Brooklyn Bridge, weaving through light midmorning traffic, skirted the Brooklyn waterfront, and pressed ahead to the Expressway and the Gowanus Parkway.

Felicia sat huddled near the window, staring straight ahead. She'd taken off her shoes and folded her knees to her chest, clutching them to her as though for comfort.

Nikki thought about the ten million dollars Douglas had stolen. People had been killed for much less. Where had the money gone? Roger Roth wanted to find out, too.

Suppose Felicia was lying about the money—that she'd known all along what Douglas was doing. Wouldn't she have told her father? What would Garcia have done for a chance at ten million bucks, a mountain of gold?

They raced along Gravesend Bay, passed a few lonely fishermen casting out into the gray water. The closer they came to the motel, the more Felicia seemed to shrink into herself. When they got out in the parking lot she looked like a doll with wide, frightened eyes.

The chambermaid had come by the time they arrived. Her cart stood in front of the laundry area next to Garcia's room, filled with linen, soaps, plastic ice buckets. Nikki found her inside the laundry room, a young Indian woman, holding a fresh supply of towels.

Nikki showed her badge. "I want you to open nineteen."

The girl stared at her, terrified, the towels shaking on her arm. She set them on the cart, fished in her pocket and handed Nikki a ring of keys, holding up the correct one.

The lock was stiff. Nikki had to jiggle the key to get it to work. She hoped against hope that Garcia would cry out from inside, ask who it was. When no sound came, she felt her stomach twist. The door gave suddenly and opened with a single push.

She smelled it right away—blood mingled with stale tobacco. She didn't have far to go to find him. Near the bed the muddy maroon swirls of the carpeting had grown larger, brighter, blended into a single crimson blotch. Garcia lay at the center of it, a ragged hole in his throat, another through his chest, his shirt stained the same vivid shade as the carpet. His eyes stared sightlessly at the ceiling.

Nikki crouched at his side, lifted his wrist to look for a pulse. She didn't need the iciness of his skin to tell her he was dead—she'd guessed it the minute she'd seen him.

She became aware of a thin, piercing wail from behind her. Felicia had backed against the dresser. Even with her fist in her mouth, she couldn't stop screaming.

22

Meekins, the tall blond Crime Scene technician with the pockmarked skin, arrived in the wagon with his partner. "Really racking them up, aren't you?" he said when he saw Nikki.

Garcia had been killed during the night—Meekins guessed somewhere around two, three in the morning. "You got rigor mortis in the whole body—that would make it more than eight hours ago." Apparent cause of death, two slugs from a revolver. No cartridge casings again. Was it the same gun that had killed Sunmann?

Kevin had heard no loud noises, nothing unusual during the night. But Garcia's room was the one farthest from the office, and Kevin wasn't the sharpest kid. He had his head in the TV most nights. He might have heard the shots and thought they were noises on his program or a car backfiring on the parkway. Garcia had been the only guest at the motel. The nearest house was blocks away.

She left Bernardi in charge of the crime scene. She'd left a message for Lawton but so far she hadn't heard from him.

Bender was waiting outside the door of 19 like an anxious poodle. "What a mess!" He bobbed alongside as she walked to the office. "This is the *worst* thing that ever happened to me."

"It was pretty bad for Mr. Garcia, too."

"Awful for our reputation! Why here, anyhow?" He sounded as though he expected her to know.

She opened the door of the office. The relief clerk, a young black girl, had a call on hold for her.

It was Lawton. "What's up?" he asked.

"Garcia's dead—couple of bullet holes in him."

"What! What happened?"

"I came out here to check on him—"

"Why?"

"It's a long story. I had an idea about Douglas—how he'd tie into the Sunmann murder."

"Didn't you turn the Douglas thing over?"

"No." He'd advised her to, but she hadn't. Though it was irrational, she felt she was to blame for Garcia's death—if she'd done what Lawton had said, this might not have happened.

He paused. "Look, I'll clean this up as fast as I can and come over. The guy in the duffel bag case is singing like a canary—giving us the whole bit, stuff only the perp could know."

He sounded happy. For one unreasonable moment Nikki resented it. "Garcia's daughter's here," she said.

"What's she doing out there?"

"That's part of the same long story." She felt like an idiot, as though she'd been ignoring basic detective work, playing long shots and hunches instead of doing her job.

"Hang in," Lawton said, "I'll see you later."

She went to find Kevin. He sat behind the desk, head propped on an elbow, eyes half-closed. He'd asked to be allowed to go home when the relief clerk had come, but Nikki had wanted to talk to him again.

"Did you hear anyone come in last night?"

"Nope."

The murderer didn't have to announce himself. Maybe he—or she—hadn't even pulled into the parking lot. Could have parked blocks away and slipped past the office on foot.

"How about phone calls?"

He bent to check the record sheet, his hair falling forward stiffly. "He didn't get any. He asked me to make two."

He handed her the sheet so she could see the numbers. One was Arden's, the other his home number in the Bronx.

"When did he make these?"

His eyelids drooped. "I don't know."

Bender piped up from behind her, "You're supposed to mark the time, Kevin, you *know* that."

"I forgot."

"Never gets anything right," Bender said.

Nikki handed the sheet back to the boy. "Kevin, you told me that Mr. Garcia called the desk last night and asked not to be disturbed. When was that?"

He looked blank for a moment, then his face brightened. "Eleven-thirty. It was just at the beginning of *Horror Theater*."

"What did he say?"

"Not too much—like, 'I don't want you to clean tomorrow, I want to sleep.' Something like that. I couldn't understand him—he talked funny."

"His accent?"

"Yeah."

"Did he sound the same as he did when he registered?"

"I don't know. I didn't register him. Donna did." He pointed to the young black relief clerk. "I came in right after."

"But the voice on the phone was definitely a man's?"

"Yeah." He stared at her blankly. "Yeah, definitely."

How could he be so sure when the TV had been competing for his attention at the time? Nikki had a sudden sickening vision of making a case against the killer, bringing Kevin into court to testify, and having him admit that he was watching *Horror Theater* when he spoke to Garcia or someone imitating him.

"Okay, Kevin. I'm through if you want to go home." She turned to Bender. "I'm going to look in on Garcia's daughter."

Felicia had been resting in Bender's office. Nikki nodded to Cook, the ponytailed rookie, who stood guard outside.

She walked in quietly in case Felicia was resting, but she was sitting upright in a corner of the cracked leather couch, staring straight ahead, her eyes swollen and her skin pasty white.

"How're you doing?" Nikki asked, sitting down near her.

She shrugged. "I keep thinking how am I going to tell my mother. I keep blaming myself. Who got him the job? Me. Otherwise none of this would have happened. Yesterday when he came home he told me he was going to be rich. He'd have enough to bring up my mother and the kids. But I shouldn't say anything to anyone. Especially I shouldn't talk to you, to the cops—I could get hurt. Who could hurt me? I asked. 'Felicia, don't tell what you know—nothing.' And then we heard you come. He ran down the fire escape. Afterward I thought—what do I know? What was he warning me about? The only thing I could think of was the Spanish lessons, and that didn't seem important."

Nikki leaned forward, not sure she'd heard her.

"I was teaching Barry Spanish, since August. He made me promise not to tell anyone. Two nights a week we stayed late at the office and I helped him. He was getting pretty good. Everyone thought we were having an affair. That was part of the deal—I couldn't tell anyone."

Nikki remembered the Spanish dictionary she'd found on the shelves of the Douglas library, the verbs in the steno book. She'd assumed it was someone learning English. She felt something quicken in her.

"That was the only secret I knew. He paid me good money, so I kept my mouth shut. Fifty bucks an hour."

Nikki stood suddenly, said, "Thanks."

"I don't understand what my father meant. I—"

"I'll explain it later. Go home and rest."

Nikki burst into the outer office, startling Cook. "When my partner shows, tell him I'm at the Douglas place—got it? And that I need him. Tell him to hurry."

She called over her shoulder, "And make sure someone takes Ms. Garcia home."

She raced out to the car. If what she suspected was true, she might save a life. If she got there on time.

23

She plunged into the Fury, turned the key, heard the motor roar to life. She knew now what had excited Frankie Sunmann on Sunday night, knew with a certainty, as if she'd been there. He'd come from the marina, gone straight home, and watched the news on television. She could picture him flicking on the TV, watching the reports, only half paying attention, and then. . . .

She rounded the corner on Hampton, her breath coming fast. She had to stay cool and think, had to be careful, but time was slipping away. Their elaborate farce had gone smoothly till now. Some things they'd done puzzled her; she couldn't figure out how. But one thing she knew—they'd played their game so well they wouldn't let anyone stand in their way, not on their last day—not even a cop.

The Douglas house looked deserted when she passed it. Had they gone already? She couldn't remember when Denise had said the flight left.

She parked a block away so that the slam of the door wouldn't be heard in the stillness, then hurried back along the sidewalk, unsnapping her holster as she ran. She crept inside the fence that bordered the property, looking anxiously for lights in the windows. The glass reflected only pale autumn light. If they'd gone, wouldn't they have left some lights on to make an intruder think someone was really in?

They would have set the burglar alarm before they left. She might have to break in, trigger the alarm system. If only it wasn't too late!

What if they were still there? She hadn't thought about the possible danger before, had felt only the urgent need to get here. How soon would Lawton come? He'd go to the Star Garden first. Would Cook remember to tell him to rush, that she needed him? It wasn't too late to go back, find a phone, call for backup. But her gut told her to keep going—to hurry.

It was past five. Daylight was fading fast enough to give her some cover. She edged to the end of the fence, crept to the flagstones that circled the house in a continuation of the front path. She pulled her gun from its holster now and nicked off the safety. Her heels made tiny clicking noises. She took off her shoes, leaned them against a coiled hose.

Down the flagstones and around the corner. She'd never been behind the house before. The broad back lawn spread into the dimness, disappeared at the bordering shrubs. A light flicked on suddenly. The ground floor windows threw pale rectangles on the grass. Had they seen her? She could hear every beat of her heart.

A free-standing brick fireplace stood on the patio next to the back door. She stole across, crouched behind its broad shape, and looked back at the house. Her breath caught. Arden was framed in the window, not ten yards away, her back toward Nikki. She walked around a table, lifted Brian from his chair, carried him inside.

As soon as she moved from the window, Nikki crossed the patio and flattened herself against the back wall.

The back door was aluminum, a button catch in its handle. It had to be squeezed to open it. She waited till she heard Arden's footsteps retreat into the center of the house. Every sound seemed magnified—a bird's chirp, a car passing out front, Arden calling, "Brian." She squeezed the button catch, praying it wasn't locked. It gave under the pressure of her thumb.

Inside. She ducked away from the light of the kitchen, huddled on the landing of a narrow wooden staircase to the right. When Arden spoke she was startled. She sounded near enough to touch—she must have come back into the kitchen and was now standing near the door, just out of sight of the staircase. "I'll go up there again just before we leave," she said to someone. "I'll take care of her then."

Arden was going back "up there," wherever that was. Nikki had to get up there first, before Arden could "take care of her." She looked at the dusty, winding staircase, decided to take it where it would lead. The treads were narrow and old, bare of carpeting. She inched upward, tried not to make noise. The eighth tread wobbled underfoot, sounding like the crash of a thunderbolt. She held herself rigid. Had anyone heard? She waited. No one came. She moved on again.

The steps spiraled up, ended in a small landing on the second floor. Outside she could see the balcony above the front entry. She stepped out, found herself behind the elaborate chandelier. An inner voice urged her on. If only she knew where to go!

Along the width of the balcony she counted six doors, three of them open.

Below, a muffled voice said something from deep in the interior of the house.

Arden answered, "Okay. I'm going to dress Brian now."

Did that mean she was coming upstairs to get his clothes? Nikki froze, but no one came up the broad marble staircase to her left or the steps behind her.

She had to make a move, even if it was the wrong one.

She slipped into the nearest door, the master bedroom from the look of it. Canopied bed draped in a flowered chintz, antique fainting couch done in a coordinated stripe. Clothes, papers, personal possessions strewn on every surface. The room looked as if it had been ransacked. A quick look told her she hadn't found what she was looking for.

On her way out, she saw a cylindrical box on the floor. Aunt Eleni had owned a wig when they were in style, had kept it in the same kind of box. She lifted the lid. Dark curly hair rested on a wig stand. She remembered what Kevin, the motel clerk, had said about the woman who registered as "Mrs. Amos Johnson"—"Like Brooke Shields, except maybe a little older." Tucked into the side of the box were the sunglasses that would have completed Arden's disguise as Mrs. Johnson. She jammed the lid on the box, kicked it under the bed for safekeeping, and sped out to the balcony. Where next?

Below, she heard Arden say, "Let me button your shirt."

"I want my doll Wile E. Wile E. come with me."

"Let me finish dressing you."

They sounded as though they were almost directly below, under the chandelier. She kept well back along the wall, slipped quickly into the next room. A large mural had been hand painted over the bed, a decorated rendering of the name "Brian." A giant panda sat on the blue carpeting, surveyed the disorder. Drawers were open, their contents scattered. She looked at the bed, but what she was searching for wasn't there. Just piles of children's clothing and a quilt with a huge *B* appliquéd in its center.

The third room—the guest room?—held satin-covered beds, neat and empty. A pipe stood in the corner, the heat riser. Nikki remembered Denise mentioning it.

Back on the balcony. The three closed doors. The knob

of the first turned easily. Brian's playroom. Jungle gym on the carpeting, rocking horse in the corner with its painted eyes staring. Plastic toy bins overflowed.

"Mommy, I need my Wile E. Coyote."

"Hold still."

"Wile E. come to the warm place, too. Wile E. swim in the pool with me. Wile E. come on the plane, too, Mommy?"

"I don't even know where Wile E. is, honey. I think you lost him."

"Not lost. Wile E. in toy room." Nikki whirled around but didn't see the doll in any of the toy bins. "I go get him."

"You stay here—we're almost ready to leave. I'll get Wile E."

Nikki bolted from the playroom. She had no time to decide which of the two remaining doors to open. She grabbed for the nearest. A linen closet, stacks of sheets and pillowcases. She heard footsteps on the lower stairs— Arden coming to get the toy—and crammed herself against the shelves. She could have stood her ground and confronted her—she had the gun. But the commotion would serve as warning. She wanted *both* of them. To do that she had to take them by surprise. Right now they weren't even the first piece of business—if she didn't hurry, there might be another death.

The footsteps mounted, came closer. She squeezed herself against the linen, struggled unsuccessfully to pull the door in behind her. Would Arden notice the door was ajar? Nikki's nose was pressed against a stack of sheets. Lint tickled her nostrils; she willed herself not to sneeze.

Footsteps approached, sounded hollow on the parquet. Then a heart-stopping silence—no sound at all. Where was Arden? Staring at the linen closet, thinking, *I didn't leave it open!*

Then Arden said, "Damn!" A muffled sound, not close by. An instant later her shoes tapped on the parquet again, moved down the steps.

Air flooded out of her in a rush of relief. She stepped out on the balcony.

Where now?

Arden had said she was going "up" before she left, to "take care of her." But there was no one on this floor, not as far as she could see. Could she have meant the next one, the attic?

Below, Arden said to her son, "I couldn't find it."

"I get Wile E."

"You stay here. I'll buy you another as soon as we get there."

"I want *my* Wile E."

"Brian!" warningly.

How could she climb higher? There *must* be a way.

The only other door, the one she hadn't tried, was next to the playroom. Locked. A thin key rested in the hole. She turned it, tugged, and the door swung open. Narrow wooden steps led up. Dust motes danced in the fading light.

She tore ahead, cursing the creaking stairs, her stomach twisting. Was this a dead end? It didn't seem likely they'd keep running up two flights to the attic all the time. And yet . . .

The space was large, cluttered with bulky shapes, the air thick with camphor. She became accustomed to the dimness, made out a sofa, coffee table, armoire, piles of storage boxes, plastic trash bags. The eaves sloped down on both sides. Twin dormers had been added front and back to bring the space to standing height. Insulation glimmered dully between the beams.

A bed stood in the nearest dormer, holding what seemed

to be a mound of blankets. Nikki ran toward it. Her toe
kicked something small—a mothball?—and sent it rolling.
She bent. A limp figure lay flattened among the bedclothes.

She circled the bed so she could keep her eye—and
gun—on the staircase. The bedside table held a small
lamp. She switched it on but nothing happened. Then
she saw the cord on the table. She found the outlet on an
upright beam, stooped, and plugged it in. The light came
on immediately, a sick yellow haze.

Denise lay in the bed, her skin bloodless, her body still
and unmoving.

Nikki took Denise's wrist, felt her heart lift—she was
warm to the touch. She laid her ear against the girl's
chest, heard the slow, faltering beat. Near the lamp was a
bottle of Seconal, a loose pill on a plate, a covered water
pitcher, a glass, some cotton balls.

"Denise!" Nikki whispered. She put as much urgency as she
could into her tone, trying to keep it low at the same time.

The girl's eyelids fluttered but there was no answer.

Nikki slid her free arm under her shoulders, raised
her. She felt feather light, like Lara, her body frighten-
ingly limp. "Denise!"

Something tapped behind her. She spun but saw nothing in the shadows. Mice?

Denise made a whimpering noise that made her turn
back. Her eyes were open. The whites were yellow, the
pupils unfocused.

"Can you sit up?"

"Arden . . ."

"Arden drugged you." A skilled nurse, Arden had known
exactly how to keep her sedated. "Try to sit."

"She . . . I saw him. . . ." A thin line of saliva escaped
from the corner of her mouth. Nikki wiped it with a
cotton ball. "Water—I . . ."

She let Denise's head rest on the pillow and reholstered her gun, poured a glass of water. She looked warily into the shadows behind her, then back at the stairs. Nothing moved.

Denise's eyes had closed again. Nikki slid her arm under the girl's shoulders. "Here's some water. Sit up."

She had the glass to her lips when she heard the deep male voice behind her. "Put it down and let go of her."

Shock registered along her spine. There was another staircase, another way to get up here. He hadn't been in the attic all the time. He'd been downstairs, talking to Arden.

"Don't try anything funny. I've got a gun on you." His voice was hard, businesslike. She remembered what he'd done to Sunmann and Garcia. He wouldn't hesitate to kill her.

She released her grip and straightened, put the glass on the table.

"Now turn around. Slowly."

He was standing in the shadow of a wardrobe some yards away, near the coffee table. Bigger than she'd pictured him, not heavy but taller and more muscular, powerful thighs and calves bulging in snug jeans. He was very dark, just like his photo, except that he wasn't sunburned.

Barry Douglas looked drawn and desperate, a manic gleam in his eye. His .38 was pointed straight at her heart.

24

"Move to the side, copper."

A stray thought flashed through her head—how did he know she was a cop? Then she realized Arden must have described her; he'd recognized her by her height.

"Move." He kept the gun trained on her. "Step away from the bed."

"Make it easy for you?" The barrel of the .38 gleamed blue and deadly. She had to sound confident, though her blood ran cold.

"Don't think I wouldn't use this."

"I know better. After Sunmann and Garcia one more wouldn't matter." Her breath was coming in gasps; she couldn't slow it down. "Poor Sunmann. He saw you down at the marina, didn't he?"

"Dumb jerk. He asked me for a light—I gave him some matches, and he got a real good look. Then he went home and saw me on the news. The TV says I'm dead and he knows I'm not. So he puts two and two together and becomes an entrepreneur. Calls my wife and wants twenty-five thou or he'll go to the cops."

If only she could reach the light cord. One good yank and the lamp would go out. She could grab for her gun in the darkness. The trouble was he'd pick her off the minute she moved. "So you had to kill him."

"I don't like loose ends."

"The Coast Guard guy saw you go down with your boat—"

"He saw a dummy, dressed up like me. I had to make it look real, in case the cops or the insurance people checked into it."

Instinctively, she leaned closer to the bed. "*You* were Amos Johnson."

"Who? Oh, yeah, the name my wife used at the motel."

"That whole business about your wife having a lover was just to mix me up."

"Smart. A little late, but smart anyhow. I gotta give you credit for that." He took the smallest step to the left.

Nikki noticed the movement, tried not to let her eyes or voice show she was aware. "You made an appointment with Sunmann, met him at the diner, and shot him. Then you came here. How'd you get here?"

"By bus. What's the difference?"

"You didn't figure on Sunmann—that messed you up. Otherwise you could have taken your ten million to some banana republic and lived like a king. Felicia was teaching you Spanish, getting you ready."

"Very good—give the lady a gold star! I'll go anyhow. Think anything's going to get in my way? Ten million bucks— You ever see ten mil?" He laughed. "People like you can't even think about that much money. Gives them a headache." Another tiny step to the left—why was he shifting position? "I been planning for years. No one's going to stop me."

"Not even your kid."

"What're you talking about?"

"Denise. You didn't figure she'd be home from school. You got rid of Garcia when he found out about you—you planning to whack Denise too?"

His eyes hardened to points of black steel. "You crazy? My own kid?" He moved again, ever so slightly. She saw his plan now. He wouldn't risk hurting Denise. He'd begun to swing around to get clear of her. Another foot and he could shoot. She calculated the angle.

"She's just under for a little while," Douglas said. "Arden gave her something to keep her quiet."

"When're you leaving?"

His eyes shifted dangerously. Did he see the coffee table jutting into his path at shin level? "You're too nosy. That's your problem, copper."

If he'd seen the table, he would avoid it. A little more and he'd have a clear shot with nothing behind Nikki but the staircase. Before she'd let that happen, she'd grab for her gun. If she went down, she'd take him with her, damage him on the way. It was her last chance.

"You're not as close as you were to Sunmann and Garcia. How good a shot are you? Going to take a chance on hitting your own kid?"

"You ought to zip that big mouth."

Denise moaned.

"She's waking up, Douglas. You want her to remember you as a killer?"

"Shut up."

His leg hit the point of the coffee table. Just a tap, but enough to distract him for a beat. Nikki dove wildly, yanked the cord. The room went dark.

She rolled to the side. A blast from the .38 thwanged the floor just inches from where she lay, deafening her.

Under the smoke and dust she crawled toward the staircase. A dim haze filtered up from the steps. Her ears felt as if they were stuffed with cotton. She looked for cover, crouched behind the armoire, drew her gun. The touch of its cool stock sent a shiver of relief through her. Her .38-caliber buddy.

Her hearing eased. Sound filtered through. From across the attic running footsteps on the far staircase—Arden, her voice frantic. "What happened?"

"Where's the kid?"

"Downstairs. I—" Her voice suddenly cut off.

Whispers. Silence.

Douglas was planning again. The great controller. Pushing people around, snapping their lives in two for his convenience. Rage filled her, charged every vein with purpose.

Denise whimpered low, pitifully, like a sick animal. "Rick . . ."

Then Brian's voice nearby and below, on the balcony level. "Mom?"

"I'll be down in a minute, Brian. Wait for me," Arden called.

Nikki sat still, tried to think. Two against one. Douglas and Arden knew the house, were familiar with every inch.

If she could drag things out, she'd make it. Lawton would come.

How soon, though? What if he knocked and no one answered? Would he come inside? Or would he figure she'd left already?

Brian's shoes clicked along the parquet below. "Mommy?" Closer. Sounding worried.

Arden's tone was sharper this time. "Stay there, Brian. I'll be down in a minute." Then, her voice becoming silky, "Detective Trakos? Can't we talk? Cops are people, too. They need money like everyone else."

The words burned Nikki's ears. They wanted to push their dirty money at her.

"We're talking a lot of dough, enough for all of us to be comfortable. You, your family. You could give them things you always dreamed about."

I'm a cop, she wanted to say—I protect the law, I don't break it. But plenty of cops had turned and taken payoffs, made shakedowns. Did they take her for one of those? Outrage filled her. She wanted to charge out, pistol-whip Arden till her skull cracked and her blood ran.

"We can split any way you want. Five million for you, five for us. There's plenty."

Shut the fuck up! she almost screamed. Caught herself at the last minute and realized she'd allowed her emotions to take over, wasn't thinking. Easy. You talk, you give them your position. Douglas was probably scanning the attic right now, gun cocked, listening for the slightest sound so he could nail her. Where was he? Why was Arden doing all the talking?

"Rick . . ." Denise moaned.

"No one would have to know. It would be between us." Arden sounded smooth, as though she really believed what she was saying. She was talking "payoff," but the only payoff they planned was from the barrel of the .38.

A footfall. She gripped the gun in firing position, squinted into the darkness.

A mothball skittered across the floor. As though someone had kicked it.

Nikki saw him first. Behind her. Through a gap in the scroll on the armoire's side she made out his shape— almost ten feet away. He'd taken the gun, told Arden to keep talking while he came around the side. Even the whisper of a movement would tell him where she was.

She didn't want to shoot him. In a gun duel there was a good chance she'd get blown away herself. And she wanted *him* alive, too, so bad she could taste it. She wanted to be in court the day they took his toys away and sent him up.

"Mommy?" Brian's voice drifted up again from the foot of the stairs. "You coming down?"

"Soon, honey," Arden said.

Nikki tensed herself, drew a bead on Douglas.

Clumsy footsteps sounded on the lower stairs. "Mommy, I come up, okay?" Now the boy was clattering upward, almost at the top.

Nikki hesitated for only a second. "Brian, go back!"

Arden's scream was drowned as Douglas's gun barked. Nikki's left shoulder burned with a sharp stinging pain. She held onto her weapon, ducked toward the top of the staircase opening, where Brian stood. Douglas struggled for a clear shot at her around the armoire.

"What that noise?" Brian asked.

"Over here," Nikki whispered. She grabbed him, held his small body snugly. She hated using him as a shield, but if she didn't, she was as good as dead. Douglas would take her out without a second thought. A fierce throb began in her shoulder.

An overhead light went on.

She held Brian in front of her, a kicking, squirming armful. "Let me go!" He twisted, trying to get loose. She felt as though her arm had been torn from its socket.

Opposite, Douglas trained the gun on them. Arden had come up behind him. "Barry—don't! Oh, my God!" He struggled to find a clear shot at Nikki. "No, Barry! You'll hit Brian—you—" Arden grabbed his arm.

He struck at her suddenly, hit her temple with the gun. She went down, more dazed than hurt, while he looked desperately at Nikki and his son.

Nikki felt as though someone had driven a stake through her shoulder. Blood oozed from her shirt, soaked her jacket. How long could she stay upright? Red spots danced before her eyes. She blinked them away. Had he noticed? She couldn't show her weakness. With willpower alone she kept her grip on the boy, held her gun on Douglas.

"Barry!" Arden was on her knees, arms around his legs, sobbing. "Oh, my God! Oh—don't try anything—please!"

"Put the gun down, Douglas. It's over."

He stared, disbelieving. Life seemed to drain from his face. His features withered, shrank.

"It's finished," Nikki said. "Do I have to spell it out for you?"

The boy began to cry. "Mommy—she's hurting me! Put me down!"

"Barry—please! I beg you!"

He lowered the gun slowly, pointed the muzzle at the floor. It fell with a clatter.

"Kick it over."

Her legs felt wobbly. Waves of heat passed over her, alternating with icy chills. If she passed out now, everything would be lost. They'd make sure she never woke up. Could he see how fast she was losing strength?

She held on as though her life depended on it—clutched the boy with shaking fingers. The urge to let go was overwhelming.

Douglas thrust out his foot. The gun landed less than a yard from her. Two thin tracks shone on his cheeks—tears of rage and regret.

From below she heard the sound of shattering glass. A double siren squalled.

Lawton shouted up the steps, "Stretch?"

"Here in the attic."

Relief flooded through her. She could hang on till he got here.

25

Pale autumn sunlight pushed past the blinds, dappled the maple rocker on which Lara's Couch Potato doll lay.

Nikki finished the last bite of ham and Swiss. Unfortunately, the nick from Douglas's gun hadn't done anything to hold down her appetite.

She uncrossed her legs. "I'll get the rest."

"Sit there," Lawton ordered.

"Stop babying me. It was just a graze." In the two days since she'd been hit, he'd spent all his spare time at her house, treated her as though she were made of spun glass. It was funny how fast he'd become a fixture around the place. The work on his duffel bag case had tapered off, allowing him some free time. The killer had given a full confession. Over the next weeks Lawton would keep compiling evidence so that charges could be brought before a grand jury.

"The doctor said two more weeks and I'll forget it happened," Nikki told him now.

He ignored her, walked into the kitchen. "Lara—you bringing the tea?" she heard him say.

"In a minute."

Nikki recrossed her legs, called into the kitchen, "I don't know if I can get used to sitting around." Eagle-Eye had insisted on the whole bit—the exam, six weeks' medical leave. She felt good enough to be back on duty, but the decision wasn't hers, he reminded her. She didn't understand it. He *had* to be impressed with her performance. Her first big case had been a dazzler. She'd become a legend in the precinct overnight. But there seemed to be no difference in his attitude toward her, not so far.

"What'm I supposed to do for the next six weeks?" she complained as Lawton returned.

"Gives you time to think—about dead heroes and live cowards. Like, next time you have a dangerous situation, wait for your partner."

He set his coffee on the table, sat in the loveseat. He wore frosted jeans, a wrinkled linen crewman's shirt. The patch of hair that showed in the vee of his collar was darker than that on his head, curly. No matter where else she'd tried to look all day, her eyes kept returning to it.

"I was afraid they'd kill Denise," she said. "I didn't realize Douglas wouldn't hurt his own kid till he told me that."

"Your instincts were good. They were giving Denise Seconal, but that last pill—the one on the plate—was digitalis, the lab said."

"Whose idea was that?"

"The wife's."

"That would've killed Denise, wouldn't it?"

He nodded. "She'd have been out of it in a couple of hours."

Her skin crawled. "Barry didn't want to kill Denise—there wasn't any reason at that point. All he had to do was get off the plane in Caracas and he'd be safe. He just wanted to sedate her, to give him a chance to get away."

"But the wife hated the girl. She figured if she let her live, she'd trace them and make trouble."

"Did Douglas know about the digitalis?"

He shook his head. "Planned it all by herself. The first time they gave her Seconal they ground it into a pudding she ate for dessert. After that all they had to do to get her to swallow one was put it on her tongue."

"I spoke to Denise this morning. She's better and she's back at school."

Lara came in, clutching a mug in one hand, a glass of milk in the other. "I made you Lemon Soother, Aunt Nikki. Okay?"

"Fine." She set down Nikki's tea, looked at Lawton uncertainly, then sat near Nikki, wiggling close. He didn't seem to notice.

"What happened to the bozo," he asked, "the girl's boyfriend?"

"Kerrigan?"

"Yeah." He'd been picking apart bits of the case for two days now, playing trivia with tiny details. As though there'd be nothing to say once they stopped talking shop. And there might not be.

"Turns out he's been clean all along. Denise said they figured out who owned the coke down at his job. It belonged to the janitor, the guy who accused him." The tea was too hot to drink. She blew off some of the steam, rested the mug on the sofa arm. "Denise is more worried about Brian right now. Arden's sister has him, but she can't keep him permanently. And it looks like Arden and Douglas will be away a long, long time."

"The wife started out as an accessory, but now she's up for attempted on the girl. She'll probably end up with five to fifteen. They'll throw away the key on Douglas."

"Too bad he had to take out so many people."

He sipped his coffee. "He was in a big hurry to get out of the country, to a place that wouldn't extradite to the US."

"I should have figured it out before," Nikki said, "when I first heard Douglas didn't have life insurance. I mean, what guy in his right mind doesn't carry insurance?"

"He couldn't," Lawton pointed out. "If the wife had a big claim on the insurance company they'd have investigated the explosion—maybe brought up the engine and checked it. This guy had it all planned. He took no chances."

Lara put her empty glass down on the table, the light catching her hair and turning it gold. When she leaned back again, the movement jiggled Nikki's sore shoulder, made her wince.

Lawton crossed his legs. Silence seemed to fill the room, seep in like a stale odor. A moment of it was more than Nikki could stand. "What was that whole business Garcia fed us about delivering a package?" Now she was doing it, too, stretching the details of the case, looking for the last drops of water in a stream that was about to dry up. "That story he told us about going to the motel—"

"A fake."

"I figured. Douglas must've concocted it, told Garcia to make us believe it. We were supposed to think there really was somebody else involved—"

"What was his name, Smith?"

"Johnson."

"Yeah, Johnson. A phony, like I said."

"Arden was very convincing the day she told me his name was Mitch Robler. She even had a photo of him."

"Was that a real guy?" Lawton asked.

"He sure was. She picked someone who'd been popular with the ladies at the racquet club, used a picture she'd taken of him with her friend, Marcia Breitson. This Breitson woman had actually had an affair with Robler." Her shoulder *did* ache, especially when her back was relaxed.

"I have a feeling Douglas was the brain behind the operation, told his wife exactly what to say."

"Right." She leaned forward, eased her discomfort. "But

his plan backfired. If he hadn't met Sunmann, he could have stayed at the motel."

"Yeah. The perfect plan. The wise guys would blow up the boat, then he'd hang around the motel a few days. Meet his wife on the plane and go off to Venezuela. Then he makes a little side trip, collects the embezzled dough from his Swiss bank accounts. They live happily ever after. Nobody ever finds out. Except Sunmann happened to ask him for a match."

She nodded. "And after he killed Sunmann he couldn't stay at the motel—it was too risky. He went right home. It didn't take Garcia long to figure out he was there, and he asked for bucks to keep him quiet. The day I questioned Arden, Garcia listened in. When he heard that murder might be involved, he raised the ante."

"You know, I could never understand why Douglas left Sunmann's wallet on the body, made it easy for us."

"One of our guys took a guess the first day, said it might have been too messy for Douglas. Sunmann had been"—she was going to say "bleeding like a stuck pig," changed it for Lara's sake—"Douglas might not have wanted to get dirty."

She became aware of Lara listening with wide, interested eyes. She remembered suddenly her own attention to Uncle Spyros's stories, how they'd been better than anything she'd ever read. Would Lara become a cop, too? She felt an odd mixture of pride and apprehension, a desire to protect her. It probably wasn't healthy for Lara to hear all this stuff.

"What're you going to do this afternoon?" she asked her.

She waited for the inevitable reply. The sun was shining. Kids were roller skating, building tree houses, playing ball; the whole world seemed to be young and out of doors, enjoying the last warm fall days. She braced her-

self for Lara's words—whenever Nikki was home she
would say, "I'll stay here," and sit in the house, cling like
a barnacle.

"I don't know," Lara said.

Nikki blinked, tried not to look surprised.

Lara turned to Lawton. "Could you make another boat?
You know, out of paper. I gave that one to my friend
Karen."

Her *friend*? Had Lara actually said *friend*?

"Sure."

Lara ran to get the paper.

Nikki felt the tightness around her heart ease, fade
away.

Lawton walked over to stand above her. "What are you
smiling about?"

"I thought she— I don't know. . . ."

Lara ran back in, handed him the paper. He sat next to
Nikki, began to model the boat. A mixture of after-shave
lotion or cologne and the special scent of him tickled her
nostrils. She fought her response, the feeling that wanted
to take over, wanted to fill her completely.

The boat took shape under his big hands.

Lara said to Nikki, "I thought I'd go over to Karen's
house. But if you need me—"

"I'll take care of her," Lawton said. "Don't worry."

"It's okay?" Lara's eyes were on Nikki.

"Yes, it's fine," Nikki said.

Lara grabbed the finished boat, called, "Thanks," and
ran down the steps. Nikki heard the door slam.

She turned to look at Lawton and the feeling rose in
her again, even more intensely. This time she didn't fight it.